THE Combustible ENGAGEMENT

MARIA HOAGLAND

ALSO BY MARIA HOAGLAND

BILLIONAIRE CLASSICS
Beauty and the Billionaire Beast
Her App, a Match, and the Billionaire
Falling for Her Billionaire Best Friend
The Matchmaker's Billionaire
Bargaining with the Billionaire

COBBLE CREEK ROMANCE
The Inventive Bride
The Practically Romantic Groom
The Combusitble Engagement

DIAMOND COVE ROMANTIC COMEDY
Sun-Kissed Second Chances

FOR THE LOVE OF SOCCER
Love for Keeps
Santa Cam

HARVEST RANCH
While You Were Speaking

ROMANCE RENOVATIONS
Home for the Holidays
Kayaks and Kisses

SPELLBOUND IN HAWTHORNE
Taste of Memory
Sprinkle of Snow
Hint of Charm
Dash of Destiny
Stir of Wind
Essence of Gravity

STAND-ALONE NOVELS
Still Time
The ReModel Marriage

THE Combustible ENGAGEMENT

MARIA HOAGLAND

RED LEAVES PRESS
2017

© 2017 by Maria Hoagland

All rights reserved.

No part of this book may be reproduced in any form or by any electronic or mechanical means, including information storage and retrieval systems, without written permission from the author, except for the use of brief quotations in a book review.

This is a work of fiction. The characters, incidents, and dialogue are products of the author's imagination and not meant to be construed as real.

Published by Red Leaves Press, an imprint of Sisters Ink Publishing, Kuna, ID.

mariahoagland.com

ISBN-13: 979-8842498017

LCCN: 2018903279

Cover design © 2022 by Red Leaves Press

Author photograph by Erin Summerill © 2015

Printed in the United States of America

*To my amazing sister, Michelle.
I'll always look up to you, but never again from behind a catcher's mask. The biggest compliment would be for you to finish this and pronounce it a "good book."*

Chapter One

Tess Graham led her clients, Mr. and Mrs. Perry, into the large eat-in kitchen. An old dresser had been expertly transformed into a marble-topped island, the cabinet a distressed blue that added a pop of color in the otherwise white country kitchen. The kitchen was open and airy, and pretty much every client's dream.

"Can you see yourselves enjoying family meals here? I can't think of a better kitchen-dining space we've seen so far."

Mrs. Perry walked up to the bay window and practically pressed her nose against the glass. "Oh, this is gorgeous." She stepped back, never taking her eyes from the outdoors. For all the attention she'd given the house, Tess could have found her a shack as long as it had this view. Which was fine. Whatever the client wanted. "That would be perfect for Cheyenne." She laid a hand on her husband's forearm. "I can just imagine watching her practice while I'm cooking dinner or reading a book here at the table . . ." Her voice trailed off dreamily. It was definitely a good sign.

Mr. Perry nodded his head. "Maybe . . . The stables were in great condition. Newer than most, even if they are small. And the fact that there's already an outdoor practice arena works."

Although what he said was mostly positive, Mr. Perry wasn't as easy to read as his wife. Tess tugged absently on her necklace as the two talked through it. If the view didn't clinch the deal, she didn't know what would. This house checked off more of their wish list than any other property she'd shown them so far, and she'd shown them everything in their price range. They should be ecstatic about this house. It was beautiful, secluded, updated, and under budget. What wasn't to like?

"With a space like this, Cheyenne could really get serious about her barrel racing." Mrs. Perry was starting to convince Mr. Perry. Another good sign. "If we can find the right teacher."

"You know who would be good—" Enthusiasm finally tipped Mr. Perry's words. He turned his eyes on Tess. "Aren't you Ava Graham's sister?"

He barely waited for a response, but Tess had

already nodded automatically. Of course this would come up.

"Ava Graham the barrel racing champion a few years back?" Mrs. Perry asked.

Off in his own little world, Mr. Perry shook his head in admiration. "She was amazing. The best Cobble Creek has had the past thirty years. You don't ride, do you?" He barely looked at Tess and didn't give her a chance to even respond. The question was rhetorical, as if there were no possible way Tess could be as good as Ava at anything. This was nothing new to her. Mr. Perry looked back at his wife, excited at the connection he was making. "Ava was good. Better than good. She could have gone pro, I think. I know you remember her, Fern."

"Oh, I sure do." Fern Perry placed fists on full hips, but her eyes glazed over as if she were somewhere else. An old rodeo, presumably. "Can you imagine how good Cheyenne would be if she were able to take lessons from Ava Graham?" She and her husband, at least, had a united front on this one. "Do you think if we bought this house, Ava could teach Cheyenne a few lessons?" She eyed Tess as if this were a stipulation that would be written into the offer for the house, if they wrote one.

"I heard she's coming back for a visit soon," Mr. Perry said.

That was news to Tess. She hadn't heard that yet.

Mr. Perry checked out the mechanics on the

window. Another good sign if he was looking at details like that on the house. "Do you know if she's going to work in Cobble Creek when she's done with med school?"

"I don't know." Tess was barely holding in her frustration. Ava had talked about setting up a practice in Cobble Creek, but Tess didn't feel like getting into it. It was too far away—she had her entire residency to complete first—and too personal, really. The whole barrel racing lesson idea was hypothetical, but buying the house, well, that needed to be done now, and without those kinds of strings.

She wanted to sell the house for any number of reasons, but getting the sale because she was Ava Graham's twin would chafe. What about her own skills and talents? Tess had built her own profitable business from the ground up. Last year, Tess had sold a record number of homes. Tess had a nearly perfect 4.7-star rating with her clients, amazing reviews, and excellent stats. She was dang good at matching clients with their dream forever homes. Except this time. All they cared about was Ava.

"We'll take it," Mr. Perry said, making his decision final. "Draw up the papers and bring them by my office at one."

Okay, then.

Tess was satisfied she'd made the sale, but the part about Ava still didn't set well. Except she'd get over it.

And a little chat and a hug from her dad would do the trick.

Tess Graham parked her SUV in front of her father's pharmacy on Main Street still in the gloom of Ava's shadow. Not for the first time, Tess fantasized about leaving Cobble Creek for a bigger city where people appreciated her for who she was, but her life was here. Moving was a big production, she knew, and with a healthy business she'd worked hard to build, most of her family, and all of her childhood memories, she was somewhat tethered to the area. Yet days like this made the work of relocating sound more like an adventure than a drudgery.

Tess pushed the door open, stepping from the bright sunlight into the refreshing air conditioning, and she took a calming breath in an attempt to cool off emotionally. She strode past the old-fashioned soda counter toward the pharmacy at the back of the store where she knew her father would be.

"What's this about Ava coming home?"

"Morning, Tess," Gordon Graham grumbled almost inaudibly, but his mouth kept moving as he silently counted out a few more pills. He herded the correct amount into the small plastic bottle and screwed on the lid before looking up over his reading glasses at his daughter. "Come again?"

She knew he hadn't been listening. "I hear Ava is coming home?" Tess could feel the confusion wrinkled into her forehead and tried to relax. She liked her sister fine. They rarely disagreed because they rarely talked. After high school graduation, the two had gone their separate ways. Or more specifically, Ava had gone her way—to college and then medical school—while Tess had remained behind, obtained her real estate license, and started selling Cobble Creek one property at a time. "What about residency?"

"Oh, that." Gordon turned and placed the bottle in a bin. "She's got a couple months off before residency starts, and she told your mother she might be coming for a visit. We don't know when she's coming or for how long, but your mother is over the moon about it, of course—"

"Obviously." That must be why everyone in town knew: her mother sharing the good news.

"—she has a feeling Ava's going to be getting married soon," he continued as if Tess hadn't even spoken.

"Ava's engaged?" Tess blurted out. Of course. She took a slow breath, hoping her father wouldn't notice.

"Oh, no. Not yet. But you know she and Tyler have been together for . . ."

"Five years."

"And she's hinted that this might be it." Gordon came through the pharmacy door, checking to make sure it locked behind him, and then placed an arm around Tess. "What can I get you?" He squeezed and then dropped his arm. They walked side by side to the soda fountain. "I know you didn't come down here to talk about Ava."

Her father's touch had soothed her in a way that frustrated her even more. She wanted to be mad at him, but he had nothing to do with any of this. "I was just sneaking down for a sparkling raspberry lemonade, but I can make it myself."

"Allow me." Gordon waved to a customer who walked in, and then washed his hands and then started preparing the drink. "What do you have this afternoon? A clandestine meeting?" The way he raised his eyebrows at her made her laugh.

"You wish." He handed her the drink, and she reached for a straw. "You never know, Dad. I don't tell you all my secrets, you know."

"I am well aware, sweet pea. And you know it's only because I want you to be happy."

Connie from the hair salon entered, her strawberry-tipped hair and matching bubbly personality filling up the space. "Hi, guys! I hear Ava's heading back to town, huh?"

Wasn't there anything else people would talk to her about?

A reminder beeped from Tess's phone, saving her. "Oh, shoot. Dad, I've got to run. I was supposed to drop off some paperwork in ten minutes." She turned off the alarm, shoved her phone back in her purse, and rushed toward the door. "Bye, Connie!"

Chapter Two

"Yet one more town to get to know," Johnny groused from the passenger side of Monroe Scott's old standby pickup.

If there were two things Monroe could count on it was, one, that no matter which town he and his crew was assigned throughout western Wyoming, he would be driving his slightly worse-for-the-wear pickup, its black finish matte under a layer of dirt and ash, the interior freshened by daily doses of wildfire smoke. It was the nicest thing he owned, since everything else in his life was temporary, but his vehicle accompanied him on every new adventure, every new job assignment, and the latest job assignment was across the state line and a good five hours away from home.

The second thing Monroe could count on was that his longtime assistant helitack supervisor, Johnny "On the Spot" Stein, would be grumbling about the town.

"You mean one more town we get to save." Monroe's answer was knee-jerk, but no less sincere. Something about the small town of Cobble Creek intrigued him.

Main Street stood straight forward, its shops and businesses lined up like orderly, well-maintained soldiers. Antique shops, a bookstore, flower shop, and an old-fashioned diner exuded small-town charm. The hanging planters, though, snagged his attention as each basket of flowers struggled in the summer heat, the edges of the plants singed. Town residents waved to this truckload of dirty wildland firefighters—strangers in their community—and even used crosswalks like there was some crazy-strict sheriff in town enforcing jaywalking laws. The town was a paradox.

"Diner or old-fashioned soda counter?" Monroe asked his three passengers. He didn't care as long as he got something to wet his parched throat. Who said Wyoming didn't get hot?

He was about to pass both establishments and, by the looks of it, end up on the short road out of town if someone didn't decide pronto.

"Pharmacy," one of Monroe's helitack crew, Ryan, said, leaving him barely enough time to yank his steering wheel to the right and pull into the last parking stall. "Might as well do something out of the ordinary while we have the chance."

Monroe couldn't agree more. He stepped out of his

truck and stretched his back in the hot, dry air and looked up into the mostly clear sky. Hot was relative, he'd learned. Once you've experienced a few wildfires up close and personal, a regular ninety-plus-degree day in July was nothing. In the same way a clear sky was also somewhat relative. Compared to where the fires were raging, the smoky haze in Cobble Creek was a shadow of what it could be—would be, if they couldn't get the Wolf Ridge Fire contained and out soon.

Sparked from Independence Day fireworks meeting dry forest vegetation, the simple fire had spread into a massive incident. Although not in the immediate area when it started, Monroe and his helitack crew were called in to support the growing numbers of hotshot and engine crews as the fire raged on, even a month later. Now, after their first five days on in the area, the crew had been ordered to take their day off, and they'd decided to venture into town for a break.

"You can't tell me you aren't getting tired of this, man," Johnny said, not wavering in his determined pessimism. "You've been working fires longer than the rest of us."

"I think it would be great to have some kind of distraction for when we're not on duty," Ryan said, stomping his boots on the sidewalk to rid them of the dry mud that clung to them. "I know the fires are high, but they've brought in more teams than ever this year, and—"

"Do not tell me you're complaining about not having enough work to do," Monroe cut him off. "Because I could get you scheduled for doubles."

"No, you couldn't." Ryan rubbed his hand across the back of his neck. They both knew strict policies precluded overtime, wanted or not, but as supervisor, Monroe could find other ways to make things harder on his crew members if he wanted to. "Supe, sir."

Monroe shook his head at the tacked-on respect. Underneath it all, he knew his crew respected his position as the helicopter supervisor, but they also worked together, played together, and joked together.

Days away from the wildfires were necessary, not only physically, but the stress of keeping his team alive versus balancing keeping the forests and surrounding homes safe was mentally taxing every moment of every shift. Each life was important, be it tree, critter, or human. But Ryan was right. As a construction worker and wood reclaimer in the winter months, Monroe was always on the lookout for his favorite kind of distraction, and on the drive in, he'd seen just the side project.

"'Graham's Pharmacy and Old-Fashioned Soda Shop,'" Johnny read the sign as he opened the door and held it for the crew. "Just tell me they have good old-fashioned Mountain Dew. That's all I ask." He bowed slightly and waved a hand in front of him, gesturing the guys to go through.

Before he even walked through, Monroe heard

voices from the inside, some local chatting to another, talking about someone named Ava coming back to town, and Monroe felt the familiar stab of loss in his gut. He missed being known in town, having a neighbor ask after his family or running into an old schoolteacher or coach.

At least he had his crew. They'd become his family over the past five years—even to the point of receiving middle-of-the-night phone calls to get them out of trouble.

"Just don't wreak havoc on Cobble Creek like you did the last town, okay, Johnny?" Monroe ribbed his buddy, eyes locked on Johnny's as if daring him to come back with a jab of his own, as he stepped over the threshold.

Next thing he knew, he'd run into someone, and automatically, his hands shot out to steady the person. A sharp elbow accompanied by a high-pitched squeak and the light scent of orange blossoms told him she was female, but he hadn't been prepared for the beauty that was practically in his arms when he looked down. "Whoa, where's the fire, pretty lady?"

Ugh. *Pretty lady*. He mentally rolled his eyes. Now that didn't sound sexist. Hopefully the beautiful redhead would take it as it was meant—a surprised and harmless compliment.

"Excuse you." The tone was all ice. "You might want to watch where you're going." She raised a cup and straw to pink lips, and Monroe distracted himself by wondering how she'd kept from dumping the drink all over him. Something to be grateful for.

"There was smoke in my eyes." Monroe offered his best smoldering, teasing smile, but the ginger beauty didn't even look him in the eye. She seemed to take in every detail of his and his friends' appearances though, and with the crew shirts, she had to get the reference he was hinting at.

"There must have been for you to assume you could park there." Why the woman needed to sound so snooty, he wasn't sure. His only crime had been to crave an ice cream soda. And walk through a door without looking first.

The woman's cobalt eyes cut to his truck, and Monroe turned to see what she meant. He still didn't see anything, especially not what she seemed to think was right before his eyes.

"None of you look handicapped to me."

He squinted for what she was talking about, but saw nothing blue—no sign, no blue lines, nothing. Was there even such a thing as handicapped parking on public streets? Maybe she was just teasing him. The realization brought out what he'd been told was his irresistible smile. If the woman was challenging him, he'd just won.

"It's n—" He stopped when he spotted the dented, rusty sign almost completely hidden by a hanging pot of peat moss and burnt flowers sharing the same post. Not a speck of blue and partially obscured, it wasn't his fault he'd missed it.

"You might want to get your eyes checked by the new town optometrist." She thumbed over her shoulder, pointing vaguely down Main Street. In front of the businesses, Monroe saw park benches, a clump of antiques cluttering the sidewalk in front of one shop, and several more of the dratted potted plants out to trap other unsuspecting newcomers to town.

"Would that be Ava?" Monroe wasn't even sure what made him ask that, but he was thrilled when it threw her off guard.

"How did you . . . ?" She swallowed whatever she was going to say, and her panicked question quelled under a new confidence. "No, I meant Dr. Wells." Her pale expression blushed hot, and he wondered what the big secret was, but he decided to spare her the embarrassment, whatever it could be.

"Yes, ma'am." He'd meant it as a joke, rubbing in the fact that she was sounding so dang bossy—which made her feisty and irresistible at the same time. She didn't seem to take it as one, though. Instead she straightened her back, threw her long, wavy tresses over her shoulder, and fought her way through the rest of Monroe's crew. "Excuse me."

Monroe ripped his eyes from the woman's shapely retreating form and to the crew who stood, as shocked and confused as he was. "Come on, guys." He motioned with his head toward the open door and the icy air conditioning spilling from it. "Let's get those drinks."

The door hadn't even completely closed before Johnny shot off his mouth. "Yeah, the smoke must have been in your eyes if you didn't see that hottie coming a mile away." He laughed. "Did you seriously think I was holding the door for *you*?" He laughed again and scratched his beard.

Monroe shrugged and looked around him. It was the strangest shop he'd ever seen. Mostly set up like a miniature pharmacy chain, there were rows of medicines and beauty products, candies and flats of bottled water. At the back of the store, a window opened into the pharmacy where Monroe spied prescription bottles waiting to be dosed per doctors' instructions and at customers' requests. What made Graham's unique, though, was the front corner of the store. Perpendicular to the street-facing glass window was a narrow 1960s boomerang-pattern Formica counter, edged in corrugated shiny chrome. It had to be the original, real deal.

"And that smoke must have clouded your mind if you didn't notice how judgmental she was," Monroe shot back to Johnny. The woman might have been pretty, but she was way too goody-two-shoes for him.

With a couple sitting at the table by the window playing a card game and looking like they very much wanted to be alone, the men settled into three of the five chrome stools fronting the counter.

Monroe didn't have time for snooty people like her. She had no place to judge him. So he hadn't seen the sign. And he couldn't very well go out and move his truck with her watching—though it was taking every ounce of restraint to keep him from doing so. He didn't want to showcase the rule-follower in him. That had to be his fatal flaw, didn't it? He took a glance out the picture window, waiting for her to leave. As soon as her fancy SUV left its spot behind his and she was out of sight, he would pull his truck back. Until then, it would be hard to relax. Some cop could show up any second.

"I'm not here to meet women anyway," Monroe grumbled, and even to his own ears, he sounded as if he were trying to convince himself. "I'm here to put out fires."

"Aren't we all? But a little spark's fun once in a while too, you know," Ryan said. "And you two snapped."

Monroe blew out a breath. The guys were full of it. The only thing that snapped between Monroe and that woman were tempers.

"Of course, if you aren't interested . . ." Ryan knew he didn't need to finish that sentence for Monroe to know what he was not-so-subtly hinting at.

A protectiveness Monroe had no right to have reared up. "I don't think she's your type, Ryan." How could Monroe justify that? If anyone went after her, he wanted to be the one, but it wasn't practical. Not when they'd be in town for a couple of months at most, and then they'd be back across the state line and up the road several hours with no reason for their paths to cross again.

"Oh yeah? How's that?" Ryan challenged him.

Monroe was about to respond when their conversation was interrupted.

"What can I get you fellas?" the man in the white lab coat behind the counter asked. While the man's words sounded appropriately polite, there was an edge to his jaw, a hardness to his bright blue eyes so startling against his nearly-white hair. "This isn't exactly the place to be hitting on respectable young women or disparaging them either."

"I'm sorry, sir." Monroe wanted to tell the guy it wasn't any of his business, but his parched throat insisted he not get kicked out of the establishment just yet, especially when a root beer float was on the line.

Their silence settled for a moment, effectively changing the subject.

Monroe continued, "Old-fashioned soda shop, huh? Is it like all those new soda shops cropping up with the different flavor combinations?" Monroe worked hard to keep his opinion of the sickly-sweet concoctions from tainting his comment in case that was exactly where he'd walked into.

The man laughed, his shoulders relaxing as he got a

hold of himself. "Those places have nothing on me—I can fix up anything you ask for—but I've got way more than that."

"Ice cream?" Monroe asked, hopeful.

"How about the biggest Mountain Dew this side of the Montana border?" Johnny cut in.

"Got both." The pharmacist, Dr. Graham, it said on his coat, walked around the counter and pulled a large foam cup from the stack. "Straight up?" He lifted the cup to Johnny. "Are you sure you don't want some vanilla ice cream mixed in—make it a snallygaster?"

"Snallygaster?" Johnny echoed.

Monroe slapped the counter in front of Johnny. "He'll take it," he ordered, and then addressed his longtime work friend. "With a name like snallygaster, you gotta at least try it."

Johnny looked up to the ceiling and huffed, and then looked over at Ryan on the other side of Monroe. "This is all your fault . . . 'Try something new,' you said." Johnny was the biggest grumbler of all time, but he was all sharp edges with no cut. He didn't mean a thing by it.

The man stood, cup raised, waiting for Johnny's approval.

"Fine," Johnny barked out. "I'll take the snally . . . whatever."

Which meant it sounded good to him.

Putting back the foam cup, the man grabbed a stainless-steel cup and got to work. He blended the drink and slid it in front of Johnny. "And the rest of you?" He raised his eyebrows in question.

"Root beer float." Monroe couldn't wait to extinguish the fire in the back of his raw throat. Even after nine seasons' worth of breathing wildfire smoke all day, he still struggled with dried out sinuses in a serious way. He didn't even want to think about the damage he was causing to his lungs.

"Cherry Coke and ice cream, all mixed up like his?" Ryan pointed to Johnny's drink, nearly a third of the way gone already.

"Want a shot of chocolate in that?" the man suggested.

"Sure. Why not?" Ryan was true to the whole trying-something-new idea.

"Red Brown Cow it is." Dr. Graham turned and began assembling the drinks. "How bad's the fire?"

Whether buttering them up to make regular clients of them or concerned about the safety of his livelihood, Monroe didn't much care. The man had a right to know, but Monroe didn't want to scare him either. "That's what we're here to take care of." And Monroe was certain they would. "Nothing for Cobble Creek to worry about, honestly."

The man slid the blended ice cream soda across the counter to Ryan at the end, landing it expertly in front of its requester. He'd clearly done this a time or two.

Ryan took a long draft of the red brown cow before digging in with his spoon. "It's probably good that Monroe's blind considering he doesn't deserve her anyway."

Was Ryan still stuck on the subject of the woman Monroe had crashed into? Not that he blamed Ryan, but Monroe wished he'd forget about her already.

Monroe's eyes had been trained on the man creating his drink and couldn't help but notice the shoulders and neck stiffening again as if he were trying to listen in. Why was he so interested? Then again, bartenders liked to be in the know, right?

"Monroe's too much of a maverick to care," Johnny agreed.

"What do you mean by that?" Monroe accepted his drink gratefully and dug in. He wondered if he should be offended. Why wouldn't he be just as good for that woman as anyone else?

"Just that you never get serious about any of the women you date when we're out working the fires," Johnny said.

"Women are just a distraction." With Ryan's singular focus on his drink, it was difficult to imagine him paying attention to any woman.

"To you." Monroe took another drink, allowing the creamy coolness to soothe his throat and his temper. "I'm never in a position to stick around, so it's not fair to get serious. We travel wherever the wind blows us—or wherever we're told to go—and I don't need anyone sitting on the sidelines worrying about me. And neither do you, so I suggest you forget about her."

That was all he wanted to say on the subject, but Monroe already had the feeling he wouldn't be able to get the woman off his mind. Even without his crew's encouragement, he already hoped he'd run into her again—well, maybe not so literally next time. Except maybe he didn't. Sure, she was pretty. And feisty. But the way she butted into his business, told him what he was doing wrong, he didn't need that.

"Hey." Monroe needed a way to interrupt this conversation before it went south. "When we're done here, do you guys mind if we take a detour on our way back? I want to check out this old barn I saw as we drove into town."

"Another barn." Johnny wasn't surprised. And he shouldn't be. They'd done this in many of the other out of town trips before. "Sure, why not. If you buy me another of these for the road." He lifted his stainless-steel cup in toast to Monroe.

Chapter Three

Tess Graham closed her eyes for a few moments, allowing the breeze to float around her, lifting locks of her hair and weights of impatience from her shoulders at the same time. She breathed in deeply, expecting the comforting scent of pine and earth, but it was laced with wildfire smoke, reminding her of the run-in with the wildland firefighters outside her dad's pharmacy. But Tess wasn't going to let it bother her anymore. She had driven out of town for an escape. An escape that happened to coincide with work.

Tess attempted to look around her grandfather's property with an objective eye. There were benefits to knowing a property when she was the listing agent, but there were also distinct disadvantages as well. This particular piece of land outside Cobble Creek held a special place in her heart. It was the setting for some of her very favorite memories. So many family barbecues had taken place here, lawn games and fishing, but the best was learning to her grandmother's palomino, Buttercup, when she was nine. The new feeling of freedom and independence was heady at that young age.

Riding with Ava had been the highlight of every week, a treat for having completed another week of school and checking off Mom's chore chart with no arguments, until she overheard Uncle Gary and Aunt Marlene talking about them. "Tess is a good rider, and with practice, she'll get better, but Ava . . . she's a natural." At that, the appeal evaporated. While it hadn't been the last time she'd ridden, it had been the last time the two of them had ridden together. After that, any time Ava asked to ride, Tess found a reason not to.

That was the beginning of where they were now—with the rest of the town knowing Ava was coming home for a visit, but Tess being in the dark. Her relationship with the property was just as complicated at the one she had with her sister. Ninety-eight percent of the memories she had with her sister were treasures, but sometimes it was hard for her to see everyone else moving on with their lives while she was stuck in a rut.

Determined to get over it, Tess retrieved her camera from the backseat of her SUV. She had been tasked with listing the barn and its gorgeous acreage, and despite her sadness in parting with the property, she would do her best to fulfill the responsibility.

Tess lifted the camera to take pictures; focusing on the real estate assets minus the sentiment. A small stream bubbled along the edge of the property, feeding a line of trees that ended in a small grove. Long grasses fluttered in the wind, fringing the white fence slats that shone in the sun. She captured what she could, but focused on the barn.

She started with a few full-building shots from a couple of angles, and then went in for some closer ones. It was different than shooting a house, considering the barn didn't exactly have much to differentiate inside without distinct rooms like a kitchen or great room. One of the biggest selling points would be the updated plumbing and electricity, not to mention a good solid concrete foundation. It had been built to last, but nothing lasted forever without at least a little TLC. Still, all it needed was the right person, someone devoted to rehabbing the place. There was plenty of room on the parcel of land for a house to be built and still have room for a yard and a horse pasture.

Tess unlocked the padlock on the barn doors and let the chain dangle from one handle. She threw both doors open wide and stared into the cool darkness. The silence inside went beyond calm, almost to creepy, but Tess was sure she was alone. Dust motes swirled in the light she'd allowed to flood the atrophied barn. It had sat fallow for several years now—pretty much ever since Ava exchanged her barrel saddle for a college desk—and was worse for the neglect and wear of the harsh Wyoming weather. Tess clicked on the power switch and the overhead lights hummed to life with one lamp about two-thirds of the way back flickering angrily. At least Grandpa had remembered to turn the power on again.

Tess stepped in, awed by the high-peaked timber frame of the agricultural cathedral. As an adult, the massive exposed posts and rafters reminded her of Gothic churches, but as a child, she had pretended it was her very own castle. Fifteen years later, she appreciated details like the rough elegance of the hand-shaped beams high above her head, and the rich patina of the old boards bathed in memories. With a little imagination, this could be a unique home with way more character than most of the ones bought and sold around Cobble Creek every day, but there again, it would take way more work and TLC than she could ever give it.

Resigned to fulfilling her duty, Tess took scores of pictures. The L-shaped barn housed various-sized rooms from horse stalls to small tack rooms and a large carriage room. A generous hayloft opened up in one corner of the vaulted ceiling, but the ladder was long gone. Probably for the best, since she didn't want Grandpa or her real estate company to be responsible for curious buyers who fell to their death or dismemberment. After a few close-ups of the water hookups and drains, she finished with the interior and flicked off the lights.

Tess only needed a couple more pictures of the barn from behind, and she'd have anything she could possibly need for the listing. She walked slowly around the western corner, not wanting her excuse for being out there to have run its course. Was her grandfather selling the property for the money, or was he just tired of paying taxes on a property he rarely used anymore? If he just wanted to be rid of it, what would he think of her buying it? But could she really justify such a purchase for sentimental reasons? And realistically, what would she do with a barn that was falling apart?

How surprised she was when she rounded the corner to the same three she'd met just an hour or two before. Two of them—had she heard any of their names?—had a tape measure stretched between them, debating about holding it steady and on the corner.

"Stop yanking. You're not getting the sag out of the tape, you're just pulling me off my mark," one complained.

A third man had his back to her, his fingers shoved underneath one of the corner boards and wiggling it back and forth until the whole board gave way. Seeing that lit a match within her and she located the number for the sheriff's department and pushed the call button before she had time to think about it.

"Cobble Creek Sheriff's Office, Judy speaking. How may I help you?" The dispatcher's voice had a practiced calm to it.

Tess winced. This probably wasn't the best use of this line. She wasn't in any immediate danger, was she? They hadn't even seen her yet, and they hadn't seemed menacing before.

"This is Tess Graham." She was surprised to hear her voice shake, but it made sense considering they'd caught her completely off guard. Honestly, she couldn't believe she hadn't heard them arrive. How quiet could three men in a diesel pickup be?

She stepped back from them, but didn't want to duck back around the corner, deciding that keeping an eye on them was the best idea. "I'm out at Roy Graham's stables on County Road 122. There are four trespassers here vandalizing the property."

The one closest to her—the cute one she'd run into at the store—looked up at her, first with surprise, but it quickly evolved into an angry glare. "Vandalism?" He scoffed at her concern.

"I don't know these men. They aren't from Cobble Creek. And . . ." Tess wondered if she should even pursue this. If the men meant any harm, they could easily have cornered her inside the barn a long time ago. But she'd gone this far already, and it didn't hurt to ask for a little backup. "Could you have the sheriff come out?"

The man raised his eyebrows and his eyes grew wide just for a moment before he dropped the now-loose board to the ground. He took several steps back, raising his hands as he backed off. "Why did you do that?"

The man obviously wasn't going to hurt her, and Tess considered canceling the whole thing. In fact, she'd opened her mouth to tell Judy *never mind* when the man shook his head and turned away. "You're absolutely ridiculous."

"Miss Graham?" Judy's words brought Tess's attention back to the phone. "I've alerted Sheriff Lockheart, and he should be out shortly. Please stay on the line until he gets there."

"Thank you, Judy." Tess smirked back at the pompous firefighter. Oh, he'd asked for it. "What are you doing here?" she directed at him rather than into the phone. She narrowed her eyes for a fraction of a second to show she meant business. "No one is supposed to be here."

"You are." His retort was so quick, it had to have come from reflex.

"Smoke must be in your eyes again, because this is private property. You might notice some big differences between it and downtown areas, shops that vie for your business, open parking lots for your"—she glared at his truck once again as she had done earlier—"gas guzzler." They were both lucky her stares didn't cause his pickup to spontaneously combust.

"I didn't see one of those 'posted' signs."

The smart aleck, a wisecrack about the handicapped sign, she supposed. If only there had been one, but that would have been too good. "There shouldn't have to be. People don't have to post them at their homes, why should they have to at their barns?"

"How was I supposed to know this was private property without a sign?"

Tess huffed. "As if it would even matter to you. You seem to have a knack for ignoring signs and breaking laws around here, don't you?"

The guys behind him laughed, and the one holding the tape measure retracted the tape. Apparently, Tess's conversation with rebel-man was more interesting than getting the exterior measurements of a dilapidated barn. What she couldn't tell was if they were laughing because they were on her side or his.

Emboldened, Mr. Ego took a step forward. "Do you have any idea how much this barn is worth?" With that one small burst of encouragement from his cronies, Tess's confronter had gained confidence enough to challenge her, it seemed.

"Precisely what I am doing here, actually." Tess stepped toward him. She was in the right, after all. "I am a Realtor. It's my job to make an assessment of the fair market value." As much as it pained her to realize, here was a potential buyer right here in front of her. "This particular parcel of land will go for a pretty high price. Not too far outside of town, developed and useful. A barn with all the amenities."

"Except for structural integrity. As a building, it's a liability. A definite hazard." The man acted as if she'd asked him a question, but she knew all about this—surely more than he did. When he continued, it came out almost as a taunt. "I should think you'd be happy to get rid of the eyesore."

Tess looked at him, hands on hips, finally putting together the reason that these men were out here. With a tape measure.

"Do *you* know what this property is worth?" She threw the same question right back at him, assuming he might actually have an almost reasonable answer. Reasonable for him anyway.

"Let's just say you have no idea how much I can sell these weathered boards for. Especially since they're gray." He closed his mouth, obviously done speaking, and shoved his hands in his pockets. The muscles in his arms and chest flexed, their ropy definition highlighted with the golden tint of a suntan. She had no idea what he was getting at, but he sure was handsome doing it. After too long a break for her to answer the easiest of questions, he explained, "I run a reclaimed wood business."

"Reclaimed wood? What even *is* that?" The term was probably obvious, but then again, it was better to assume nothing. "If you're referring to this gorgeous barn"—okay, that might be stretching it a little—"it is most definitely claimed."

With the perceived slight on the structure, Tess looked up at its widow's peak rising into the crisp, blue-gray air, weathered wood standing firm after several decades of her family's use. If she remembered family lore correctly, it was her family who'd built it in the first place. Giving it up was like giving away her grandparents' legacy.

The man raised an eyebrow. "This place hasn't been used regularly for years—that much is obvious. I wouldn't call that claimed." He raked a hand through his dark hair which was in need of a trim. "But reclaimed wood is taking weathered wood such as old barns, fences, etcetera, to be used decoratively somewhere else. Generally, designers will use them on interior walls in residences and businesses, building furniture, that kind of thing. It's recognizing the value in something someone else is throwing away."

Oh, so the ugly rustic look? Mentally, Tess shook her head, rolled her eyes, and gagged all at once. *Another bandwagoner.* That look was way overdone.

"So you're a scavenger?" Although she knew the term would be inflammatory, she hated the idea of him picking apart this barn for his own gain. A buyer was one thing, but could she allow someone to purchase the property if he planned to destroy it?

A flicker of anger crossed his face, but he breathed in

deeply and exhale before answering, and she felt a twinge of admiration at that.

"You say scavenger, I say savior." The twinkle in his eye said he was challenging her.

Fine. She could do that. "You're not saving anything, you're trying to destroy it. I'm the one who wants to preserve my cultural heritage."

He stroked his chin, his eyes scrunched as if forming a way to explain his thoughts. "To me, reclaiming wood is less about selling a product for interior design. I could care less about that. Well, except that it does make a pretty decent profit. But it's more than that. Reclaiming wood is also a way of keeping our world safe . . . and tidy. Kind of like thinning the forest of dead trees. You know, old wood just lying around is one match away from a community's destruction."

There were so many things wrong with what he was saying. At least when it came to her family's barn and property. It wasn't an eyesore. It wasn't a fire hazard.

Remembering how he'd collected himself before answering, she consciously decided to do the same. She needed to go back to her first goal when she arrived that day—to look at the property as an unattached observer and a successful Realtor. It wasn't an eyesore . . . yet. It wasn't a fire hazard . . . yet. But it would be both, and soon.

Looking suddenly disconnected from the conversation, he stopped and stared at her so intensely, she wondered if she had dirt on her face. Instinctively, she pulled her hair over her shoulder, trying to fix any windblown locks. Yet the gaze felt less critical and more curious.

At last, he stepped forward, hand outstretched. "If we're going to keep running into each other, maybe we should be introduced? I'm Monroe Scott, and you are?"

Oh, he left that open for something snarky like "Not interested," and though she tried, she was unable to snuff the impulse entirely. "Running into each other? Aren't you following me?"

Monroe chuckled and seemed ready to refute the accusation, but turned to face the popping and crunching of tires on the gravel driveway. Finally. Took him long enough. Had Tess been in any real danger, Sheriff Lockheart would have been too late to prevent the worst.

The sheriff's pickup pulled in next to the other vehicles. It was starting to look like a regular party out at the Graham ranch. Sheriff Lockheart stepped out, his boots shiny against the dusty lane, and ambled over to Tess.

"Afternoon, Tess." He tipped his hat to her and then turned to the men. "Boys." His gaze turned back to Tess, but he never placed his back to any of them. "I understand you invited me out here. You've got some trouble?"

"It's just that, speaking of invited, these gentlemen

were not." A wave of hot embarrassment hit her. She was acting like a first-grade tattletale.

"So then, they're not clients of yours or hired by the owner to do some work around the place?"

Tess shook her head firmly. She'd come this far, after all, and even if she was in no danger, that didn't mean it wasn't uncomfortable being out there in the boonies, alone with four strong men she didn't know.

"I'm going have to ask you boys to leave." Trent popped a toothpick into the corner of his mouth and then gestured toward their truck, waiting.

Monroe, however, didn't move. He turned glittering blue-gray eyes on Tess, all mirth gone. "You seriously called the cops on us?"

"You had to have heard me." Tess held her ground.

"I thought you were faking it, trying to scare us into leaving." Monroe no longer looked amused, but she hadn't been trying to entertain him, or even get him to like her. She'd been trying to get them to leave, not make an enemy. Whatever. She'd never see him again after this. Even in a small town, twice in one day was already coincidental.

Monroe focused on the sheriff. "I'm sorry. I had no idea she was scared." He shook his head sadly. "I should have seen it." His eyes cut to Tess. "I'm so sorry I put you in this situation." He took a few steps toward his truck. "Come on, guys. Let's leave the lady in peace."

After opening the driver's side door, he hesitated.

"So sorry." He held up his hands again, and Tess couldn't help but think maybe under all that joking around and tough-guy routine, maybe he felt bad about it after all.

Sheriff Lockheart and Tess watched the men load into their truck and drive off, a swirl of dust in their wake.

"You okay?" The sheriff had kind eyes, his concern about Tess's welfare sincere. Why was it the best guys were already taken? Not that Tess could begrudge her old friend Jessie—they made the cutest newlywed couple since Benny and Darcy—but someday, it might be nice to have a hero of her own.

"Yes. I'm fine." If you didn't count the sucker punch of her grandfather intending to sell the land and barn. But what did she expect when, as long as she could remember, she'd been looking for a way out of Cobble Creek? She had no right to feel possessive of something she'd written off years ago.

"Did they do any damage?" Sheriff Lockheart slowly walked around the structure, searching for signs of recent changes.

"Not much. Mr. Scott removed a board that was probably loose anyway." Why was she excusing him now?

"And the interior?" Sheriff Lockheart stopped in front of the doors and the secured chain and padlock.

"They didn't get inside. I was in there when they showed up, and they were outside."

"Doing what?"

"Measuring."

"Measuring?"

The way he said it made it sound so innocuous. She was being ridiculous. No, being ridiculous would be pressing charges or pursing anything legally. She still stood by her decision to call for backup. Having Sheriff Lockheart show up added an ease and confidence she didn't have when she was outnumbered.

"It's all fine now. Thank you. They just surprised me, that's all."

"Okay. You don't want to press charges for trespassing, then?"

Tess shook her head. "No need. It's all good." They walked to their vehicles together. "Thank you for coming out here, sheriff. I appreciate knowing you're around."

She opened the driver's side of her Pilot and slipped in, but kept the door open so they could finish their conversation.

"Of course," he said, his hand on her door. "I'll keep these gentlemen on our radar while they're in town, but you make sure to let us know if there are any more problems."

"Will do." She gave him a smile and closed her door. She had wanted to spend a few more peaceful moments out here alone, but the sheriff seemed to be waiting for her to go before he did—probably keeping her safety in mind in case the men were just waiting for him to leave before coming back. She lowered her window and waved. "Thank you again."

"No problem. Have a good day."

Chapter Four

Monroe dropped his laundry sack onto the floor and settled into one of the molded plastic seats that ringed the laundromat. It had been a long and grueling week on duty, and he was looking forward to his two days off to recuperate and clean up. He gave himself exactly ten seconds to sit down, but then jumped up to load the washing machines. Untying the bag, he dumped his rumpled clothes into one of the rolling metal baskets so he could separate them into light and dark loads. Even though he wore protective clothing when he went out on the job, everything—even the supposedly "clean" T-shirt and shorts he slept in—attracted at least some soot and even the microscopic drops of tar that got into everything. He knew from experience that while the clothes would come out cleaner, no matter what, washing wouldn't pull the smoke smell from the cotton fibers. The best he could hope for was semi-clean linens with a hint of smoke as his personal fragrance.

Going through the change tray in his truck had provided at least enough quarters to get the wash going, but he'd forgotten he'd run out of detergent last time, and he couldn't start the loads without soap to at least try to get things clean.

Leaving his sorted clothes, he exited the laundromat and stood at the doorway looking both directions for the best possible option. He took a few deep breaths in an effort to clear his head. He'd had a low-level smoke-induced headache for two days straight, and while the air in Cobble Creek wasn't exactly in the green air-quality range, he could do a light yellow. It far exceeded the thick pollution at base.

A luxury SUV drove past, and Monroe found himself checking to see if it was Tess, distracted from his quest to find detergent. He hadn't seen her in a week and a half, and he wasn't sure if he was looking for her so much as looking out for her. Sure, she was beautiful, but he got the feeling she didn't so much care for him. Surely there were other women in town if he wanted to cultivate a romantic interest. He shook the thought out of his head. After the last time of getting his heart tromped on, he'd already promised himself he'd stay away from such things. A work schedule like his was bad enough when he was in town with five days on at a time, but it was awful for relationships when he had to be away for months at a time.

Knowing, if nothing else, Graham's Pharmacy was at the end of Main Street, Monroe started down the street. Surely between here and the pharmacy, there was some kind of bodega that would carry a small box of laundry soap.

"I appreciate the offer." Monroe overheard a woman talking. She had to be just around the corner from him, down one of the side streets. The somewhat familiar voice continued, "I won't be able to, though. I'm really busy. I have something planned."

By now, Monroe was convinced the woman was Tess, and a tightness in her words didn't sit right with him. He hurried around the corner, despite the fact that last time he'd seen her, she'd had the sheriff run him off.

Tess stood, feet planted slightly apart as if prepared for battle. The fierceness in her eyes counteracted the stiff smile on her lips. She wasn't looking any too kindly at the arrogant man who stood over her. Either Tess harbored a severe distrust of men and somehow Monroe had just been lucky enough to be thrown into the same category as this poor fellow or she just plain didn't know how to read them. Whether warranted in this situation or not, Tess clearly wasn't comfortable.

The man took a step toward her, not even noticing Monroe as he turned the corner. "You need to eat lunch. I need to eat lunch. Even Ava says we're perfect for each other." He reached out and wrapped a beefy hand around her thin bicep. Although her facial expression didn't change—on the verge between distaste and politeness—Monroe noticed she flinched when the man touched her. His mind went back to that day when she'd called the sheriff on her. She'd been scared and vulnerable then, and he felt awful about it, and he couldn't leave her in this position now.

"Oh, here you are, honey." Monroe took three sure steps to Tess's side and threaded his fingers through her hand hanging at her side. "I'm so sorry I was late. It took a little more time driving into town than I anticipated."

Monroe was relieved that Tess didn't pull away from his touch. In fact, she reached over with her opposite hand, pulling her arm from the other man's grasp, and slid her hand up his forearm and smiled up at him. It melted a bit of his resolve to avoid women. If he hadn't known that look was completely fake, he wouldn't have been able to resist.

"Thanks again, Glenn. I appreciate the offer, but . . ." Tess raised Monroe's hand, clasped in her own. "Well, you understand."

Monroe allowed Tess to turn him away but couldn't help but make sure Glenn bought into the situation—especially if that meant he could finagle lunch with a beautiful woman. "Are you ready for lunch? I'm starving."

"How did you know?" They were almost a block past the street where Monroe had picked her up, and Tess still hadn't dropped his hand, even when they turned the corner out of sight. He was happy to take full advantage of it as long as it lasted. Besides, they had no idea if the man was watching them.

"Know what?" Monroe hoped she wouldn't follow that up with *that I was there* because he really didn't want to be accused of stalking again.

"Know that I didn't want to be with Glenn." *And that she would accept his help*, he read into it.

"I heard you tell him no, but he was pretending not to hear." They were in front of a place called Tony's Diner. "Are you serious about lunch, because I could go for a bacon burger right about now."

Whether it was the challenge of trying to get Tess to soften up around him or the fact that he liked her tough indifference bordering on disdain, sharing lunch with her sounded like a decent way to spend the next hour. And if someone stole all his dirty, smelly clothes from the laundromat while they waited, so be it. "Have you been here before? Is it any good?"

With a confident head toss, Tess threw her fiery hair over her shoulder. "It's the best." She dropped his hand to reach for the door, but he hurried to pull it open for her. "I really do have something to do, but I have a few minutes for a quick lunch," she acquiesced, and they found a table near the window. "As long as you aren't offended when I run off. I have some clients coming in from out of town and they said they'd text when they got here."

"No problem." Monroe ordered a Sprite and accepted a menu, even though his stomach had already decided. "Did you?"

Tess looked up from her menu, eyes scrunched together declaring her utter confusion. "Did I what?"

"Want to be with—did you say the creep's name was Glenn?"

"Well, no." She tipped her chin as if to peruse the menu again, but her eyes didn't leave his.

"But you do know him?" Why was the woman so blasted difficult to talk to?

A blush creeped up her neck. Was he making her nervous by watching her or was that some kind of answer to his question?

"Fine. Don't tell me. I don't care that much, but a simple thank you would suffice." He couldn't keep from squeezing a drop of gratitude out of her, at least out loud. Her body language at the scene told him right off that his gesture was appreciated.

"Thank you." The blush tinged her cheeks now, obscuring the super-cute freckles he loved with her bright blue eyes and coppery hair.

"Of course, Tess." He was serious. "Any decent guy would do the same."

A tall guy with a man-bun walked to the table

holding their drinks. "Hey, cuz." He didn't try to hide that he was giving Monroe a warning glare. "Who's this?"

"Eh, just some riffraff I picked up on the street. I think his name is Monroe or Manuel or Marmaduke or something." As she teased Monroe, her lip quirked up a little on the right. It was adorable.

"So . . ." The guy was obviously asking if the two of them were on a date, and Monroe was relieved when Tess made no indication either way. After a moment of silence, the guy continued, "Did Jenn get your order already?"

When Tess said she hadn't, he looked at Monroe first so he ordered the bacon burger that had his mouth watering already. "The usual for you, Tessa?"

She glared at him and then let out a quick laugh. "You know me too well, Anthony."

"Fried zucchini will be up first, then Cobb salad it is."

She smiled her thanks, and he took off.

"Is he really your cousin or was he just calling you that, you know, as slang?"

"He really is." She swirled her blackberry lemonade with her straw. "Been cousins our whole lives."

He chuckled. "I should hope so. I might have worried if you'd said *practically* your whole lives."

"I guess that *would* be a problem." A ding came from her purse, and she dug her phone out to check the text.

"Those your clients?"

"Yes." She stood, and grabbed her purse in one hand and clutched the glass of lemonade in the other. "Sorry about lunch." Tess turned her back on Monroe and his world suddenly felt colder.

"Mind if I ask you a question before you go?"

She turned back, and with her smile, the warmth of the sun returned. She raised her brows. "Mind if I don't answer?" Her smile, however, said she didn't mind.

"Where's the best place to get laundry detergent around here?"

She rolled her eyes. "I can't believe you have to ask. Graham's Pharmacy, of course."

"Oh, yeah." Duh. He watched Tess reach behind the counter for a foam cup, dump her drink into it, and snatch a lid from the stack by the register. She left a crisp ten tucked next to the register, but Anthony managed to grab it and push it back into her purse with a smile and a shake of his head.

"I'll have your fried zucchini and burger out in a second," he called to Monroe over the muted din of the other diners.

Tess paused at the door and waved to Monroe, and his lunch never tasted so good. Cobble Creek was a pretty great town—even if he wasn't interested in a relationship.

Chapter Five

Tess allowed the door to Tony's Diner to close behind her, cutting off the sound of quiet, friendly conversations. Anthony always had her back, and she appreciated it—even when he didn't need to worry. There was nothing going on with Monroe. He was transient. A good-looking transient with manners who'd been her hero today.

Over the couple of years that her sister had been dating his best friend, Tess had had to spend more than one miserable evening in Glenn's presence. Their last interaction had been a one-on-one date that he'd seemed to enjoy but she'd found excruciating. Perhaps she hadn't been clear enough that night that she didn't want to spend more time with him, but hopefully today she'd conveyed that message. The scary part was that he hadn't seemed to be listening. The more he pushed, the more she pushed away. Thank goodness, Monroe had intervened.

It had been an awful year for Tess and men, and she needed a break. First there had been Logan Wells, the optometrist she'd mentioned to Monroe when they first ran into each other. Soon after he'd arrived in town, a mutual friend, Frankie, had set them up. Things had been fine between her and Logan—slow-going for sure, but not awful—until it was obvious that Frankie wanted Logan herself. Of course, the worst part about it was that Logan preferred Frankie as well. Tess could see she'd lost that one, and bowed out gracefully, she hoped, only to then have the longest dating dry spell in her life. It seemed pretty much every eligible guy in town was either related to her or not interested. But no matter how parched that spell, there was no way she'd ever allow Glenn to break it. She'd dry up and blow away before then.

Her mind slipped into the stormy whirlwind of those awful dates with Glenn she had thought were well behind her. Since she hadn't really wanted to date him to begin with, nothing ever happened between them. Truth be told, she hadn't really given him a chance, and after today, never would.

The real question was how Glenn happened to be in Cobble Creek to begin with. The man had no real ties of his own to the community. His was more of a six degrees of separation thing: he was Tess's twin sister

Ava's boyfriend Tyler's best friend—if that wasn't confusing enough—their introduction and interaction derived solely from Ava's need for double dates when the sisters got together. Like Ava and Tess no longer had a relationship between the two of them independent of men or other family members to act as a buffer. It was depressing, really.

Wait . . . Glenn was in town, did that mean Tyler, and therefore, Ava were as well?

If that was the case, that Ava was back in town, how was it possible no one in town had informed her, or that she hadn't seen a glimpse of Ava up on the town's pedestal? Anthony, who knew everything going on in Cobble Creek because of his diner, really should have said something.

She walked the few blocks back to her office to grab the fliers and comps she'd printed out for the new couple and texted them the address of the first house. Meet you there in ten minutes, she finished.

❁

Lucky for Tess—and she would never in her right mind ever say this ever again—the couple she was showing houses to had a toddler with them. Because they were good enough to keep the kid corralled, the two adults were exhausted after seeing only three possibilities, and decided everyone had earned a break.

Tess couldn't agree more wholeheartedly, seeing the wisdom in letting them go, but also excited to drive out to her parents' place to see for herself if Ava was in town.

Sure enough, Ava's sporty car sat gleaming in the roundabout of her parents' drive. Tess barely turned off the engine before Ava ran out to greet her.

"Tess! It's been ages." As if that were Tess's fault. Ava leaned in to give her a hug. "Guess what? I think Tyler's going to propose while we're here!" she whispered into Tess's red hair, a couple shades darker than Ava's strawberry blond.

Of course Ava would get engaged first. She beat Tess at everything else—starting from those few minutes' head start she gained by being born first. Tess had been playing catch up since. Ava had learned to pedal their trikes first, dive first, scored the first run in softball. Ava had passed her driver's exam first, gotten the first college acceptance letter, and graduated with a slightly higher GPA with its corresponding slightly higher class rank. She'd even left home first when Tess was still trying to figure out where to go. Cobble Creek wasn't exactly Tess's favorite place in the country, but she did have a decent job she secretly loved, and it was all she knew.

Tess shouldn't have been surprised that Ava and Tyler were on the cusp of getting engaged. They had, after all, been together through the last three years of medical school, so it probably shouldn't have been a shock, but the certainty in Ava's tone made Tess curious. "What makes you say that?"

"The one good thing about Glenn following us around everywhere we go is that I'm able to overhear things. This time it was Tyler saying he wants to take me to the top of the world. I even heard 'special gift' and 'flowers'—is there still that flower shop on Main?" She cocked her head and looked Tess over. "Well, Glenn was useful when we needed to double." She elbowed Tess and waggled her eyebrows. Sometimes for a twin, she didn't know Tess at all.

"Wouldn't you rather the proposal be a surprise?" Tess would. The man of her dreams planning a surprise romantic proposal. Yeah, you couldn't get better than that.

"Oh, no way, no! Plans. You know me and plans." Ava preened in the reflection on the hood of Tess's SUV. "You?"

"Totally. Love should overtake you like a wildfire." The mention of fire brought with it the memory of the handsome firefighter from only a few hours before. His strong jaw peppered with dark stubble. His brooding, evergreen eyes. The comfortable set to his very defined shoulders and chest and forearms. Tess reluctantly tried to wipe the image aside to concentrate on what she was saying. "I love proposals were the bride is completely blindsided. He picks out the ring, the whole deal."

Ava laughed. "There's no way we're twins. Should we go ask mom again?" Ava linked her arm through Tess's and started walking to the sweeping front porch overlooking their mother's well-kept yard. "Was that how it is with you and Logan? Did you fall desperately in love at first sight? Oh, I can't tell you how excited I am to finally meet your Logan."

Tess wanted to remind Ava to breathe, but this was classic Ava, and probably the reason she tended to be on the quiet side herself. Especially when the two of them were together. "He's not my Logan." Wow. She really should talk to her sister more. Tess stopped her sister on the porch, not wanting to be overheard inside the house.

Ava leaned over the porch railing, looking down into Mom's red geraniums. Was she embarrassed? "That makes it easier for you to hang out with us. You and Glenn can pal around again. You do remember Glenn, don't you?"

Yeah, from only a few hours ago. The taste was bitter on her tongue. It wouldn't be enough to tell Ava that she wasn't interested in Glenn, not unless she had someone else in the wings. Ava would try to convince her that Glenn would only be a way for them to pass time as a foursome and that it didn't have to be serious. But the creeper had actually managed to make her nervous, and for that, she resented him. Peace washed over her at the memory of Monroe coming to her rescue.

"Actually, sis, you and I have a lot to catch up on. I can't go out with Glenn because . . . I'm engaged."

Where had that come from?

Ava's beautiful pale blue eyes went wide. Tess had shocked her almost as much as she'd shocked herself, and she tried not to take offense to the fact.

"Engaged?" Ava squealed and grabbed Tess's forearms and jumped up and down, forcing Tess to bounce along with her. After a few hops, Ava calmed down enough to drag Tess to the porch swing for a conversation. "And it's not Logan? Who is he then?"

Regret burned in the back of Tess's throat. "You don't know him yet." Was it too late to change things? Why hadn't she just told Ava Glenn was a jerk and left it at that? Why was she so stupidly competitive with such a sweet sister? It made her feel even worse.

"I want to meet him!" Ava bounced the swing up and down like a little girl. "I can't believe you didn't tell me first."

Oh, no! Was Tess going to have to tell more people? She pictured the whole situation spiraling wildly out of control. There was no way it could end well. She regretted saying it already, but how could she back out now? It was way too embarrassing to admit she'd lied to her sister.

Tess took a deep breath and smiled. She could get out of this. "You are the first to know, Ava. And please, please don't tell anyone. We haven't really made it official." She waved her hand. "No ring, and he hasn't even spoken to Dad yet." Tess grasped Ava's forearm, her mind scrambling for a solution that would contain this without it becoming an all-consuming disaster. "You aren't going to be here long, so maybe we should wait and make our announcement to the family together."

Which meant she'd have to tell her family. Her stomach sank. Where was she going to scrounge up a fiancé who Ava didn't know? She loved her sister, but being twins, they'd always been compared—who was smarter, prettier, better at this or that. Even the people in the community talked about Ava like she was the one who got away. And she was. But that meant there wasn't a guy in town who wouldn't know and prefer Ava. With that one slip of the tongue, Tess had landed herself smack-dab in the middle of the impossible.

Chapter Six

The first thing Tess needed to do after leaving her parents' house that afternoon was to find Monroe. She had to beg him into being her fake fiancé before he heard it from someone else. Immediately after telling Ava, she'd realized there was no way to contain this issue. Bad news was hard to contain, but sometimes good news was even harder.

Tess drove down Main Street, realizing she knew very little about Monroe Scott other than he always ended up wherever she was. And he liked old barns. Where did he and his crew stay? Probably at some kind of base camp near Wolf Ridge, but she really had no idea where that might be or if she would be permitted anywhere near the site.

Not seeing his black pickup anywhere, she headed back into Tony's for the second time that day, desperate. After glancing around and finding none of the firefighters, Tess intercepted Anthony on his way back from delivering a tray of food to the boisterous teenagers in the corner booth.

"Here to ask after the guy friend you left stranded?" Anthony scratched something on his order pad and stuck his pencil above his ear. "He seemed to take it well. You might want to keep him around."

Feeling encouraged, Tess almost asked Anthony to leave a message for Monroe, but then realized just in time that if they were a "thing," Anthony would assume that Tess already had Monroe's number.

"Did he happen to say where he was going to be later?" Wouldn't she already know that if they were engaged? Ugh. That top was spinning faster… "I wanted to surprise him." She was getting way too good at this lying thing, but then again, she'd have to get even better if an engagement charade was in her future.

Anthony shrugged. "Nope. Didn't tell me anything, but if I see him walking down the street or something, I'll text you. Yeah?"

Tess gave Anthony a half-hug. "Thanks. You're the best."

"Don't you forget it." He gave her a half wave with his order pad, but she could tell his mind had left their conversation long before this.

If he was in town, where else could Monroe be? A reminder pinged on Tess's phone. "Oh, the clients." She couldn't believe she'd wasted so much time trying to find Monroe.

They had told her earlier that they wanted to grab some lunch, spend some time at a playground with their little guy, and let him nap before getting together again after dinner. Originally, Tess had planned to show the couple a few more houses, but when she'd been with Ava, they'd texted, requesting a second look at a house she'd shown earlier in the day instead. That meant her evening might be shorter—and more productive—than she'd planned. She was all for it.

When she pulled up in front of the house again where she'd previously left the Wilsons that morning, Tess's vehicle was the third on the curb, and she parked right behind the elusive black truck. Why would Monroe be here? The colliding of her two worlds made no sense.

Tess stepped out of her SUV and straightened her skirt. Had she known how long and involved this day would turn out to be, she probably would have chosen some nice slacks, but then again, in the late July heat, a skirt had its advantages. She looked up to find Monroe's eyes on her. His crooked half-smile and a slight shrug in his shoulders seemed to be an apology, but she couldn't help but smile completely. Surprised as she was to find him here on her professional turf, she was happy he was here. That one act of him rescuing her from Glenn and the few minutes they'd shared afterwards helped smooth out the rough edges of their previous encounters, and she found she was happy to see him again. Especially since she'd been running around, desperately trying to find him so she could ask a favor. A huge favor. She allowed her eyes to linger on his for a moment, but then turned her attention to her clients.

"Good evening," Tess greeted the young mom, Lauren. "Did you have a good afternoon? Get to know the area a little?"

"We sure did." Lauren watched her little guy, Noah, tug on the hedges that lined the front porch. "For a small town, Cobble Creek has some adorable common grounds. I loved the gazebo and the little playground next to it."

"I'm so glad you found that," Tess said. Two men came from the side yard—Monroe and David, the young father who walked up behind his son and placed a hand on his little towhead.

"Tess, thanks for meeting us back here," David swung the little one upside-down and he squealed in delight, but his eyes and words remained directed at Tess. "I hope you don't mind that we brought someone along. We met Monroe at the park and got to talking about reclaimed wood which got us thinking . . . There was a lot Lauren and I liked about this house, but there were also a couple of things holding us back. Like that fireplace—"

"It has absolutely no character," Lauren agreed.

"When I heard that," Monroe took over the explanation, "I said I might be able to help."

Wrapping her head around the idea that Monroe was here for the Wilsons and not her was an abrupt change in direction, but it made sense.

"And we figured why not? It wouldn't hurt to get some ideas, right?" David set Noah carefully back on the ground, hands out to catch him if the little guy was dizzy and tipped over. "Should we see if we can make this house work?"

On the porch, Tess used her phone to open the lockbox for the front door key. "That's a great idea, David." As long as Monroe actually knows what he's talking about. "Would you do the work then, Monroe, or were you merely suggesting the product?"

"That's up to David and Lauren, of course, though I could. At this point, I'm here for a complimentary consult. If they like the idea, they're welcome to buy my product or hire me to do the renovation or both." Monroe held the door open for the others to go through.

"You'll be in town long enough?" She knew Monroe had been in town a few weeks already but had no idea how long a wildland firefighter typically stayed in one place. Did he live close enough to come back if his work assignment changed?

"I won't leave them in a lurch, if that's what you're worried about," he whispered defensively as he walked past her.

It was, actually, exactly what she was worried about. The last thing she needed was her reputation besmirched by trusting the wrong contractor.

"Here we are." Tess led them into the great room, though the destination had been obvious. "What do you think, Monroe?" She raised an eyebrow to him in challenge, as curious about his opinion as the Wilsons were but for different reasons.

Monroe turned his attention and his blazing smile to the couple. "Tell me what you like and don't like about this room."

"Well, to be honest, my favorite part about the house is the location and the size of the backyard." David walked to the back window as if checking that what he said was still true. "Lauren likes the placement of the rooms." He turned a questioning glance to his wife. "Isn't that right?"

She let out the kind of coddling chuckle of an adult humoring a child. "The number and sizes of the rooms are perfect, if I could get over some of the little things that aren't to our taste." Lauren ran a hand along the fireplace mantel. "It's a little too formal for us. All the white moldings, the boring gray tile around the fireplace." She looked around as if embarrassed. It wasn't like she was insulting anyone in the room. In fact, these kinds of details were helpful for Tess so she could know what to look for if this house didn't end up fitting their needs.

"I'm just not that handy with a hammer," David admitted as if it were a sin.

"And there's nothing wrong with that," Tess said. "What would you like to see instead?" Tess pressed, hoping Monroe wouldn't jump in with solutions until the Wilsons offered some.

"Monroe described the trend to face the fireplace with old wood . . ." David trailed off, and Monroe picked up the thought.

"You two liked the idea of covering the tile with some kind of rock—which is easy enough to do on a fireplace with this shape. In fact, a couple of ideas come to mind." Monroe pulled out his phone and started searching until he found a couple of photos he showed them. "Something like this would be nice." He swiped the screen. "Or like this."

Tess wished she could see what he was suggesting, but what mattered was that the Wilsons looked pleased.

"We could figure that out the specific products later," Monroe explained, "but yes, I could do this for you, if you want, or if you know someone else, I'm sure they could as well. For the mantel, I suggest a heavy, scarred beam, probably stained darker to stand out, but that depends on what you decide for the flooring. Above the mantel, we add the planks. I have several colors and styles of reclaimed wood that would look great installed in a running bond." Tess noticed Monroe winced slightly, a tightening around his eyes when he realized he'd probably lost him with the lingo. "Instead of straight boards all the way across, we'll place occasional seams as we take the horizontal boards all the way to the ceiling."

Tess liked his recovery.

Monroe turned around slowly, taking in other aspects of the room. "It would be easy enough to switch out the window trim and substitute similar reclaimed wood there." He pointed as the thoughts occurred to him. "And a faux beam at the top of the cased opening between this main living area and the kitchen. We wouldn't want to overdo them throughout the home, but just those few changes could make a significant difference." He paused, letting the ideas settle around them like construction dust. "Thoughts?"

Husband and wife looked at each other, but it took less than a couple of seconds for them to nod in agreement.

"That sounds beautiful," Lauren said, obviously impressed.

Tess had to admit she, too, was amazed. Monroe's design ideas sounded perfect, if you liked that kind of look. One of the things Tess disliked about many of the homes in the area were the cookie-cutter aspect of the houses, but what she hated even more were DIY projects gone wrong. Ill-planned and sloppily executed projects made her cringe and run straight to the courthouse to check if they filed city permits. Now if Monroe could deliver quality workmanship with what he just described, it would certainly be an improvement. Either way, it sounded as if he might have sold a house for her.

"Wonderful." David clapped his hands once and then rubbed them together. "When can we get together to talk about products? Maybe you could draw out something for us?" Monroe nodded as David continued to speak. "We'd love to have you do the project, but what if you get called to another fire?"

"Don't forget we still have to make an offer on the house and it usually takes a month to close." Tess didn't want to dampen anyone's excitement, but the way the three of them were moving forward, at least one person had to ground them in reality.

Monroe ran a hand through his thick, wavy hair, dark as soot. Tess could tell he wanted to do it, and who was she to yank the opportunity from him?

"I'm sure Monroe will do a great job. He could always start it, and then, if he gets called away, there is a family of brothers here in town who do all kinds of reno projects. I'm sure we could get them to cover if necessary."

Monroe dropped his hand from his hair, relief settling onto his features again. "I've got plenty of before and after photos of my work." Which probably meant references too, if it came to that. Monroe nodded.

"You're going to like it, and this will be a great home for Noah to grow up in."

The little guy himself chose that moment to lunge forward, hands outstretched.

Before anyone else could react, Monroe jumped in front of the toddler with a silly face, wiggling his outstretched fingers. "You can't pass me," he said, "unless you get past the tickle monster." That was when Tess realized Monroe had just prevented the child from exploring a delicate-looking vase on a side table. Good move.

The child giggled and ran behind Lauren who smiled. "What about the beams?"

The beams on the vaulted ceiling had been painted white and blended in with the ceiling color. For the life of her, Tess couldn't figure out why someone would to do that—except that trends in color tones cycled in and out along with everything else.

"I could do the same thing with those beams as I suggested with the opening between the rooms," Monroe said.

"That would be lovely," Tess jumped in.

The couple stood soaking in the room, and Tess felt satisfaction cloak around her, knowing the sale was pretty much a done deal. The Wilsons had that look only Realtors saw. Akin to the *a-ha* look a teacher sees in a student's eyes when they finally grasp a difficult concept, Tess's favorite part about being a Realtor was seeing that "at-home" look on their faces. Lauren and David definitely had that.

"Is there anything else in the house you'd like to take a second look at?" Tess asked.

Being cautious, the Wilsons examined everything more closely this time, opening cabinet doors and checking the insides of closets. The tour ended with a discussion on the specifics Tess would present to the seller.

"I'll get the offer written up tonight and email it to you. As soon as you e-sign it, I'll present it to the seller." Tess made sure the door was locked behind everyone and walked the Wilsons to their car. "If you have any second-thoughts overnight, don't hesitate to call. I can always bring you back through, find out answers to questions, whatever." Tess waved bye-bye at the adorable chubby boy strapped in his car seat. "But I don't think you'll feel that way. What a great house this will be for your little family," Tess assured Lauren. "This is a solid house in a good neighborhood, and Mr. Scott here will help you put your own stamp on the place." She smiled up at him, and touched his forearm, a quiet request for him to stay behind.

After thanking Monroe and exchanging numbers—with Tess trying to memorize the ten digits in the right order, the Wilsons drove off.

Either Monroe had gotten her hint or he had something he wanted to say to Tess, because he hadn't even made a step toward his truck by the time the little family's car had curved away from sight.

"That was fun." Monroe's self-congratulatory grin was contagious, but Tess held herself back from celebrating just yet. While it was nice to make a sale in one day instead of stretching it out over several outings, she'd had way too many house contracts fall through before the sun went down, and she didn't even have a written agreement yet.

"It was," she agreed. "Your ideas will help spruce things up for sure. The house is way too vanilla right now." Though she would never suggest those changes for someone getting ready to list. It was better to offer a blank canvas rather than something so taste-specific.

"Vanilla is not your kind of home?" Monroe seemed genuinely interested.

"Mine?" Tess was so used to finding what other people wanted, she almost never got asked her personal preferences. She didn't often put much thought into what she would do with a certain house, other than that she wanted something . . . well, completely different. "No, not really."

He waited, so she filled in the blank.

"This house has good bones. It could be interesting with some work, but it's not my style. Someday I want something really unique." Tess put her hands on her waist and looked above Monroe's head, picturing the homes she loved. "I see so many houses that after a while, they all start to look the same. I mean, don't get me wrong, I love houses. All of them. If I didn't, I wouldn't be in this line of work.

"Even after all these visits, opening a new door is like starting a new book—you hope to be touched by each individual one. Each decade has a specific look, like each genre has specific expectations, but each structure has something new to share. It is so much fun for me to match clients with the right house."

She was talking too much, and she knew it. Well, at least he would see where her passion lay. "Though I have noticed Cobble Creek has more than its share of ranch-farm houses and cabins decorated in wood and rock and accented with bears or moose." She laughed, trying to keep things light.

"Not a fan of bears or moose then, I take it?" Monroe shared her light-heartedness.

"They're fine, if I'm on vacation in the mountains—which I never am since the mountains are my home—but every day? Eh, maybe not so much." She shook her head. "It's not me."

She eyed Monroe who was dressed in a button-down shirt and fairly new-looking jeans today. His style was completely different from that first day she'd met him. That day, he'd been in what she had to assume were the clothes he wore under his protective gear, a t-shirt and some rugged pants. Tess prided herself in judging a client's tastes based on a few moments spent together, but with this man, she found she had absolutely no idea, an intriguing realization.

"What about you?" Maybe he was a bear or moose fan, and it would totally be okay.

Monroe shrugged and leaned against Tess's SUV. "Oh, I've never really thought about it myself. I'm out so much, a permanent home hasn't been much on my radar."

"Huh. Doesn't that get old?" The question slipped out of her mouth before her brain could finish warning her away from asking. She should have been moving the conversation to why she'd been looking for him earlier in the day. She waved her hands in front of her to erase the question. "Never mind. Forget I asked that." She swallowed. "What I really need to ask is . . ." She sighed loudly and started over. "I need a favor."

"It seems like I just did you one."

She couldn't help but smile at his quick witted-ness in referencing the house sale. He hadn't even paused to plan the comeback. "I suppose you did, but I . . ."

"Need another one?"

Obviously.

She pulled out her best puppy dog eyes. "I can get you in touch with more clients like the Wilsons."

"The barn."

She couldn't read his face. Was he seriously asking? Did he understand what he was asking of her? "What about the barn?"

"How about starting with the owner's name? Broker me a deal on the wood?"

Being the listing agent on the property, it would be her obligation to broker a deal as soon as it was on the market, but it wasn't listed. Yet. She hadn't exactly been dragging her heels. She done the comparisons to figure out the property's worth and had taken the pictures to upload onto her website. But then she'd had an idea. The barn had been standing for generations. Perhaps it would qualify for historic status. She'd submitted the paperwork and was waiting to hear back. As soon as she did, the listing would go live one way or another, but if all went well, it would be under protection where Monroe or anyone else couldn't tear down the structure.

If the historic status didn't pan out, she wanted to at least try to find a buyer who would use the property as it had been intended. Someone who would keep the barn, cherish the land, maybe add a horse or two—actually spend time on the property as she herself would do. If she couldn't find that buyer, then by all means, she would sell to Monroe, but was it unethical for her to want to preserve the barn? As soon as she found out from Mayor Armstrong if the barn would qualify for historic status, she'd know if she had that protection to wield first.

Either way, in a couple of days, it would be a cinch

for Monroe to find the information for himself—without granting her a favor.

"What do you need?" He'd tucked away his teasing voice and a softer, more compliant Monroe seemed to be at her disposal.

Apparently, she'd stalled long enough for Monroe to take pity on her reluctance to offer up the barn. Now was the time.

"The thing is . . . my twin sister Ava is in town. She and I, well, we've always had this kind of not-quite rivalry between us. So when she said she was in town because her boyfriend was going to propose to her and she wanted me to hang out with them and Glenn . . ." She let the name hang on the air, and he took the bait.

"Glenn, Glenn?" Monroe stepped closer in a protective move. "As in the guy we ran into this morning?"

"Exactly." So maybe Monroe would understand. The reaction gave her hope. "When she mentioned Glenn, I don't know, my blood just boiled. I've told her before I can't stand him, but she didn't take me seriously." Tess really had dug herself into a nice little hole. "Do you have a brother? One that you, maybe, felt you had to compete with all the time?"

"Not really." Monroe shrugged it off. "I have sisters. *Perfect* sisters, so I know a little about the competition, but . . ."

"So take that feeling and ratchet it up about a million times." She hoped she wasn't belittling him, but she was pretty sure he had no idea what she had been subjected to. "I love my sister. I really do. We have a lot of fun together. But try being compared all the time and always being to one coming up second. Not only are we the same age, competing for the same friends, the same positions for teams and all that, but as fraternal twins, we didn't look the same, so we couldn't even tie on that front. For some reason, people thought it was their duty to decide which of us was prettier. Ava won on everything and just this once, I wanted to beat her to something." Tess had already said more than she'd planned. "I kind of slipped and told her I couldn't go out with Glenn because I'm already engaged."

"You are?" A confused look wrinkled his brow, and she chuckled.

"No. I'm not." She stepped closer to him; so close she could feel warmth radiating from his chest. "And that's where the favor part comes in. *Because* I'm not actually engaged—not even dating anyone—I kind of . . ."

He understood, and hopefully he wouldn't draw out the suspense any longer. He rubbed his scruffy chin. "So this is a proposal."

Oh, my goodness. Panic struck her chest. "An arrangement."

"With benefits?" There was a twinkle in his eye.

Her heart pounded. "Not that kind of arrangement, engagement, or any other kind of *-ment*." She could feel the telltale heat creeping up her chest. Embarrassment making her second-guess her decision to ask him.

He chuckled again. Probably at her discomfort this time. "That's not the *-ment* I meant either. I was thinking of how this arrangement could benefit me in other ways—like having an insider's view of town."

"Uh-huh. That's what you meant." Tess placed her hand on one hip and threw it out seductively, pairing it with as sultry voice as she could manage without laughing. "You'd like me to share the deep, dark secrets of Cobble Creek?" Her voice and posture went back to normal. "Let me save you the effort. There are none."

"I seriously doubt that, but again, not what I meant." Monroe crossed his arms and faced the sunset. "I go from town to town, yet never have the opportunity to find the unique things about it. I never get to see what it is that make people choose a town and want to stay forever."

So he was being serious. Tess mimicked his posture and leaned against the vehicle as well, glad she'd recently had her SUV washed and equally appreciative of the stunning blue and pink clouds serving backdrop to the local mountains. "I'm probably the worst one in town to do that. I'm well-known for not being much of a fan."

"Not a fan of entertainment? Not a fan of dating?" He left it open for her to finish her thought.

"Not a fan of Cobble Creek." In the silence that followed, she heard the first cricket of the evening.

After a moment, Monroe spoke, his voice barely audible in the encroaching twilight. "Really. You're a Realtor. Isn't it pretty much your job to be a fan of the town? How can you convince people to buy here if you don't believe in it yourself?"

Tess waved that off with her hand. "When people come shopping for houses, they're already convinced. I just help them find the right home."

"Hmm. I guess you have a point there. But then what is so bad about Cobble Creek?"

A flock of birds twittered their good nights in the tree off to their right. She couldn't explain. At least not right now. Her feelings about the subject were too complicated. Or were they?

"The pretend engagement would only be for a short time. You aren't here long, and neither is Ava." Tess turned toward Monroe, to convince him with pleading eyes, but as soon as she turned and ended up leaning against his right arm, the intoxication of being that close to him sent her off-balance. He smelled of clean aftershave, toothpaste, and a hint of smokiness. It was hot. "We can break up when either one of you leaves—whoever is first. Or even sooner, if you want, just please do this for at least a week or two?"

Monroe's eyes flicked back and forth between hers,

and she noticed a relaxing to his facial muscles. "Yes," he whispered, light as a summer breeze. "I'll do it."

"Thank you, thank you, thank you. You're the best." Tess grabbed his hand and squeezed lightly. "Any chance you could come to a barbecue at my parents' house tomorrow night? I'm sorry it's such short notice, and I'm sorry it'll probably be the whole family, oh this is bad, isn't it?" Tess took a breath when she realized she was sounding like Ava. "I guess it's not bad," she said a little more calmly. "I mean, you wouldn't even be coming over if it weren't for the family, right? Because it's all for show, and that's what we'll do—put on a show."

Monroe put both of his hands on her shoulders. "Calm down, Tess." He paused, giving her enough time to do just that. "It'll be fine, you'll see."

Chapter Seven

The shock of Tess's favor still hadn't worn off a day later by the time Monroe pulled up at the address Tess texted. If Monroe were to look at the variance of his impressions of Tess since the time he'd met her, he'd see a graph that jagged up and down. Ranging from mildly annoyed to completely annoyed, then to mildly attracted, and last night, straight up to completely attracted. She could have asked him anything at that point.

He cut the engine and jumped out of the truck to pick Tess up so they could arrive at her parents' together. Dating—real or imagined—was the only way he'd be able to discover if the spark he felt under a mottled sunset the night before could ignite something more. Still, he'd never imagined something like this. Fake engagement? Who thinks of a fake engagement? It seemed the definition of a red-flag warning.

After their discussion about homes, Monroe was surprised to find that Tess's house was smack-dab in the middle of a small neighborhood, barely more than one tree to a lot. The house was a Craftsman style, but new enough not to have all the character. It was neither big nor small. In fact, there wasn't anything interesting about it that he could see, and that didn't mesh with what he knew about her at all. He rang the doorbell and waited for her to come out.

So a fake engagement was a little on the crazy side. But mostly for her. It was her friends they would tell, her family she would have to explain it to. She'd be the one with the consequences down the road. If she'd actually considered all this was it really all that bad to go along with it? Why the heck not? Tess was stunningly beautiful. She had a great laugh that got better the more she used it. He could spend all day talking to her, and especially loved getting under her skin by teasing her. Being in a new town was generally quite boring, but this—this could be different. He couldn't think of a better diversion from a high-pressure job.

He rang the doorbell and shifted, looking around. The neighborhood was calm—a few kids' voices in the yards nearby, the smell of lighter fluid and briquettes as someone prepared to grill, only one car passing him, waving as the woman drove by.

"Oh, you didn't have to come to the door." Tess stepped out onto her porch holding a covered plastic bowl in one hand and pulling the door closed behind her with the other. "You could have texted."

Monroe just blinked at her. Sure some of that was because the woman was breathtaking in casual clothes. Up until the point, she'd always been dressed like a Realtor—all business-like with sharp angles and a fierceness that was both terrifying and intriguing. He hadn't been prepared for the gauzy, flowing summer blouse and linen shorts. Her hair was pulled up off her neck in a ponytail, she looked fresh, comfortable, and ... approachable.

He also blinked at her because she couldn't possibly expect him to treat her that way. "You are kidding me, right?" He waited for her to lock the door, and then accompanied her down the stairs. "Because there's no way I'm not coming to the door to pick up my date. Ever. Pretend or otherwise. If you're going to be my fiancée, I'm going to treat you like my fiancée." To prove his point, he opened the passenger-side door and waited patiently while she clambered up—which was no small feat, even for a woman almost as tall as he was—and then closed the door gently behind her. He didn't have to be head-over-heels in love to treat a woman like she was special. Even if this was just for fun, it was the little things that would make it nice.

And the thing that was making it nicest for him was the fact that there was zero pressure. There was absolutely no way Tess was going to go serious on him. No way was she was going to misunderstand him, and assume things were more serious than he really was. No way was she going to be upset when he had to move on, as he always did. He'd tried telling women before that an ending was an eventuality, yet none of them had ever wanted to believe it. But this time, Tess had come to him with this proposal and the terms. She knew exactly what it entailed. All he had to do was pretend things were more than they were, endure a few pointed questions from her family, he assumed, but hey, they didn't exactly have to be true answers, so he could make himself out to be exactly what he thought they wanted rather than worrying about disappointing anyone.

Sounded like a win, no matter which angle he analyzed it from.

By the time Monroe and Tess arrived at her parents' home a few minutes later, he was feeling much more relaxed. For one thing, they had traveled outside of town, and while Cobble Creek wasn't exactly a bustling metropolis, Monroe greatly preferred nature and the openness of country living. A product of all those years camping while on firefighting assignments, probably. Though there was the distinct possibility he'd chosen this profession precisely because he loved camping. With so many of his best memories revolving around camping with his family, it was no wonder.

Tess's parents' home was a large stucco home with stone accents and was set back from the country road at the apex of a circle drive. Wide expanses of green grass sat on either side, and Monroe was convinced either Tess's mom or dad loved spending their time driving around on little mowing tractors, because that was the only way someone could maintain such a ginormous lawn. Maybe it took both of them. Monroe felt right at home.

Tess had spent the entire ride over filling Monroe in on details he would know if they really were engaged, starting with things about her—where she went to school, music she liked, foods she detested—and he gave her the same details, but it ended up more depressing than helpful. There was way too much they needed to learn about each other to pull this off. Oh well, they could be one of those couples on a whirlwind romance. Obviously, that was the only category they fell into anyway.

Monroe barely found room to park with the rest of the vehicles. "Big party," he commented as he opened the truck door for her. He tried not to allow nerves to spoil his fun.

"If you think this is large, you should have seen us on the Fourth of July. Every Graham and extended-Graham-family member was here." She led him through the soft grass around the side of the house. "This is pretty typical for our Monday family get-together."

"This is typical?" Monroe's eyes went wide and he shook his head in disbelief. He didn't even think his family had this many people in it, and he'd always thought his was larger. "No special occasion for this party like the return of the prodigal daughter?" He hoped his humor wasn't crossing any lines.

Tess elbowed him playfully. "I don't think you could classify Ava as the prodigal. Hers might be more of the homecoming of a princess instead." At least she didn't sound bitter or jealous about it.

At the first sight of the crowd, Monroe reached down for Ava's hand and linked their fingers. It was great to have an easy excuse, but even if it wasn't real, his pulse quickened as she rubbed her thumb over the back of his hand.

"Okay, real quick. If anyone asks, the ring is coming—I'm having it specially made, so it takes a while—but . . . Is your dad going to kill me?"

Tess's Cheshire grin didn't answer his question the way he'd hoped, but before they could pursue that conversation any more, a young girl about six years old ran up and gave Tess a hug. "Aunt Tessy! You came!"

"Of course I came, Lainey. I always come." Tess hugged her back.

Lainey grabbed Tess's hand and dragged her closer to Monroe. Not sure what the girl had in mind, Monroe watched, waiting. "Who's this, Aunt Tess?" Lainey's small hand slipped into Monroe's, making him feel like a giant as his fingers wrapped all the way around her tiny palm.

"This is my friend Monroe," Tess said in that way that adults use when talking to a child.

Lainey tugged on both their hands, the bridge between the two of them, leading them into the foray of family. Hot dread dripped over Monroe like fire mix about to be lit. What if her family saw right through them? How did he even think he could pull off a fake engagement? He hardly knew anything about the woman.

What he did know intrigued him enough to want to continue the adventure of getting to know her, but still...

Aside from a few surprised looks, Tess's family acted like this wasn't the big deal he'd worried they would make it—which actually felt strange. He hoped it was because they didn't know about the "engagement" rather than a comment about his character. He blew out the last breath of worry and resolved to have some fun.

Was there any way to slip into the crowd unnoticed? Of course there wouldn't be. Even with a good forty people milling about, he'd probably be the only unknown to everyone else. He swallowed. He could do this.

As expected, as soon as Monroe and Tess neared the area with the grill and food table, a ring of Tess's curious relatives surrounded them. Sure Tess was going to make the announcement right there, Monroe coughed through a quickly diminishing airway. He could rappel off a helicopter in the middle of a raging wildfire, yet he couldn't stand the thought of twenty-five adults scrutinizing him? The fear was irrational if there ever was one.

But no one was actually looking at him. Instead, all eyes went to a short-ish man, made smaller as he hunched like a comma. Swiping his black cowboy hat from tufts of white hair, the man stepped forward, and Monroe didn't realize that that many people—especially the little ones—could be so quiet. Peace settled around them.

"Which ones are your parents?" Monroe whispered in Tess's ear, so close he could smell her tantalizing shampoo.

"Dad had to run up to the shop," she whispered back, her breath tickling his ear. "Something about one of the Gaines kids having an ear infection, so he'll probably be back before we leave. Mom is the one standing two o'clock in white capris and a red top."

Mrs. Graham was a happy woman, lovingly involved with everyone, and not intimidating in the least. She reminded him of his own mother who might even be having a very similar gathering at the family home in Spencer, Idaho right about now.

"Isn't it great to have our Ava back with us?" the older gentleman spoke. "We're so happy! And she brought her friends, Tyler and Glenn." The man swept a hand out to indicate the trio standing in a clump by the drinks.

Monroe was sure he was going to be next. There wasn't any way he could blend into the background, was there? It wasn't that Monroe was insecure. He could do this. But he was more of a background type of guy. He chose a job where he was never seen beyond his coworkers, a job when, if done correctly, people didn't even think about. He was one of many, and he was fine with that.

"And Tess brought her friend . . ." the man continued.

Yep, no getting out of this one.

". . . what was your name, son?"

"Monroe." He was pleased his voice came out strong and confident.

"Monroe," the man said emphatically, "I'm Tess's grandfather, but you can call me Roy. We're glad to have you with us. You're always welcome with the Graham clan. Unless, of course, you give us a reason to unwelcome you." The man grinned, his thick mustache quivering with what Monroe had to assume was humor. While most of the group laughed at Roy's antics, Monroe felt himself warned.

Roy called on someone to ask a blessing over the food, and the crowd dispersed, scattering for food, games, and excited conversations. He breathed a sigh of relief as everyone drifted off and he had Tess to himself.

For a moment. A strawberry blonde, her face set with determination, locked eyes on him. Obviously taking that as an invitation, she strode toward them. This *had* to be Ava. He braced himself for what appeared might be a force of nature trailed by her two male escorts like flotsam and jetsam in her wake.

When the posse arrived, Ava strangely ignored him. "Hi, Tess." She gave her sister one of those fake-looking hugs with stiff arms and enough space between them to park a tractor. Then Ava stepped back and flipped her hair over her shoulder. "Glad to see you brought *him*." As if *him* weren't standing right there. Oh, Monroe was going to have some fun with her.

"Evening, ma'am." He chuckled inside, knowing she wouldn't like anything that might make her sound old. He stuck his hand out for her to shake. "My name's Monroe. And you are . . . ?"

"Monroe!" Ava's laugh grated on him. She said his name as if the two of them were old friends. "I'm so glad you came! Tess has told me so much about you!"

He wondered what exactly that could be, considering they hardly knew each other.

"Although she didn't tell me just how delicious you are." Ava stepped toward him, uncomfortably close, and reached out both hands to grab his triceps. The touch, though clearly meant to be a compliment, held none of the tingles he got when Tess touched him. "Clearly you work out . . . or are all firefighters as fit as you?" He'd never felt so much like a piece of meat.

The more in shape the firefighter, the stronger and more trained the muscles, the easier the job was for sure. "I hear you're the doctor—I'm sure you can tell me."

Tyler shifted uncomfortably off to Ava's right side and Glenn scowled.

Ava smirked at Tess and then back to Monroe. "Yep, you're perfect for her." In Monroe's relief, Ava dropped her hands and turned to Tess. "Good job, sis. A fine choice." At least now the pretense seemed to have dropped. Ava turned back to him and linked her arm through his. "Let's get some grub." She walked that way a couple of paces, asking questions and becoming more normal as the conversation went. She wasn't as abrasive as Monroe had first thought, but she was flighty. By the time they'd filled their plates, Ava had apparently satiated her curiosity in Monroe and left him for Tyler and Glenn, who stood off by themselves. He wasn't sure if that made her flighty for abandoning him so quickly or responsible for looking after her own guests. He decided to give her the benefit of the doubt.

Tess saved Monroe a seat near the food table next to her father's brother Gary. She introduced them in a hurry, intermittently looking over her shoulder at a couple who either just arrived or were leaving. "Mind if I run off for a sec? I need to ask my aunt something."

Monroe shrugged and dropped into the folding chair. "I'm good. I've got meat." He held up his thick, juicy hamburger with all the trimmings. As if that was all that was necessary to make him happy. And as long as no one came to give him the third degree, he absolutely was fine.

Monroe and Gary settled into an easy rhythm of eating and heckling those who walked past. With adults, Monroe initiated the normal, expected chit-chat of how they were related to Tess with a follow-up question about the person's occupation. If he were a spreadsheet sort of guy, one would have come in handy right about now as he tried to remember everything and everyone. But that wasn't him. Not by a long shot.

Children and teens Monroe had a lot more fun with. He tried to begin each conversation with a different question. "Chicken or beef?" earned him a blank stare. "Cat or dog?" "Amusement park or waterpark?" and "Star Wars or Star Trek?" worked out well.

He and Gary doled out puns, jokes, and even compliments and encouragement, adding a side of humor everyone seemed to appreciate with their potluck. The whole scene reminded Monroe of his own family's reunions. He'd forgotten how much he missed being around a big family. His crew came close with the ribbing, the noise, and the sharing of responsibilities. Watching the family interact, though, Monroe realized there were a few things families took for granted that you couldn't get anywhere else—the hugs, the unconditional love, the softer side of things.

All the while he was chatting with Tess's friendly family, Monroe couldn't help but follow Tess as she made her way to a woman about fifteen years her senior. After a quick greeting, the two walked to the woman's car where she handed Tess a black strap which Tess rolled up into her hand. They hadn't even been finished with the conversation when Ava intercepted them on their way back.

As Ava dragged her past him, Tess dropped the black object on the ground at Monroe's feet. "Can you hold onto this for me?" In the toss, it opened enough for him to tell it was a nylon belt of some sort.

"What is it?" he asked.

"It's my running belt—holds my phone, a few gel packs for long runs. Marlene borrowed it for their ride Saturday."

Gary nodded. Obviously, he knew all about the belt already. "You're signed up for the Cobble Creek Hobble, right?" Gary asked. Tess pulled Ava to a stop and gave Gary a half nod. Did Monroe see her checking for his reaction with her peripheral vision? "Did Marlene tell you, she and I are manning one of the refreshment tables? We'll be handing out water at mile ten. Look for us; we'll be cheering you on!"

Tess clapped Gary on the shoulder. "I might need you more at mile twenty, Uncle Gary."

"When's the marathon?" Ava asked. "I'd love to run it with you."

"A week and a half."

Monroe saw Tess's jaw clench after she said it.

"I'm not sure a marathon is something you just jump into with no training," Gary said.

"For sure," Monroe added. "I've worked as an EMT at a couple of them, and it's not really to be messed with."

Ava waved them off. "I'm active. I keep up with my riding when I can. And you know, twenty-eight hour shifts at the hospital."

Monroe saw Tess roll her eyes. He was with her. Standing awake and spending most of that on one's feet didn't count for exercise. She was going to surprise herself

"You better get over to the croquet set before the kids do." Gary pointed to where the women had originally been off to.

Ava looked over her shoulder and obviously agreed with Gary's assessment. "Come on."

Tess followed, and Monroe almost felt sorry for her. But then, the longer he watched the women at their game, the more he realized they were having a good time together—even Tess and Ava. Playing with their mother, and a few other women Monroe assumed were aunts or cousins, the women laughed together, acting silly and basically not caring what anyone thought of them. Monroe felt right at home. Maybe this exact scene hadn't played out in his own grandparents' backyard but situations pretty similar had. A pang of homesickness hit him so hard, for a moment, he felt out of breath.

With their game over, Tess made her way toward the drink table at Monroe's left.

"Lemonade," she whispered as she dragged herself past him, exaggerating each movement as if she were literally dying of thirst. "Must. Have. Lemon. Ade . . ." She filled a large plastic cup and then fell into the seat on the other side of Monroe. "When did it get so stinking hot?"

She leaned her head back in her chair and closed her eyes, and Monroe drank in the sight of her.

"So Monroe," Gary interrupted his thoughts. "How long have you been dating our sweet Tess? How'd you two meet?"

In his peripheral vision, Monroe took note of Tess's subtle straining. She was obviously trying to listen while appearing like she wasn't. That was one vital story they hadn't made up on the drive over. It was such an obvious question, why had it not even occurred to him?

"We met through a mutual friend." Monroe's eyes flicked to Glenn, Tyler, and Ava who nursed their own cups of liquid refreshment on the opposite side of the yard. Okay, so the word *friend* was stretching it a little—Glenn hadn't even acknowledged Monroe the whole time he'd been there. The timeline was a little skewed as well considering he and Tess had run into each other twice before Glenn brought them together. While he wasn't sure he wanted to give Glenn credit for the meet, it was a safe story and not too far off the truth.

"Mutual friend, huh?" Uncle Gary mused as he watched over the crowd. "A good way to meet. If that friend actually likes you." He chuckled at his own joke, as if thinking of all the ways something being set up by someone who didn't like you could go awry, which now that Monroe thought about it, he realized could be many.

Monroe shook his head. One thing was for sure, Glenn didn't like him. Monroe could tell that much from the gold-plated cold-shoulder treatment he'd received from the man. Monroe could deal with the guy's jealous retaliation, especially if Glenn didn't do anything violent. In fact, Monroe sort of deserved it for lying to the Grahams. But he did love having Tess by his side if that meant he could give one more barb to the scrawny, entitled nerd. No matter what had been their relationship in the past, Tess didn't owe the guy anything. No woman ever owed the kind of thing Glenn seemed to be expecting.

"Well with that reasoning, I guess he liked me plenty because she's definitely worth it."

Gary clapped Monroe on the shoulder. "Good answer, son, good answer. My brother will be happy to

THE COMBUSTIBLE ENGAGEMENT

hear it." His grin couldn't have been wider if Tess were his own daughter.

"Whew!" Monroe made a show of wiping his forehead and leaning back into his chair. "So I passed the test then?" Monroe was only half-joking.

This wasn't Tess's dad—which was a good thing since Monroe had some ground to make up after the unwitting glib remarks about Tess in the pharmacy—but maybe this conversation with Tess's uncle would get a good word back to Mr. Graham. Shoot! He should have been more careful instead of joking around like a little kid all evening.

"Don't worry, this was only a test. Had it been a real emergency, you would have known." Gary leaned back in his folding chair.

"You're talking there would have been sirens and instructions and stuff?" Monroe joked.

"Something like that." Gary got up and stretched. "How are you with ultimate Frisbee?"

Monroe wasn't bad, and was temporarily tempted, until he saw the older man who'd welcomed everyone off by himself. He stood near a small peach tree at the back end of the yard, looking off across the pasture. "Rain check? I wanted to take a moment to introduce myself to a few more people."

"Be my guest." Gary jogged off to where a couple of the older kids were tossing the Frisbee. Not bad for a man who looked to be around retirement age. Monroe only hoped he'd still be that active when he reached that time of life.

Monroe took off on a slow walk around the perimeter of the party. If Grandpa Graham had lived in the area long—and generations of the family living here in the valley certainly seemed to indicate that he had—then he might have some leads for Monroe and his reclaimed wood business. The man probably knew everyone around—and their property.

The Grahams were like any big family, and just like his. Monroe looked about as he walked, sizing them up. He could pick out the leader of the kid cousins, hatching up some kind of devious adventure game and organizing the troops. Blood relatives were recognizable by their looks, but the group welcomed everyone. No "outlaws" here. After a few pleasant stops and starts to chat with a curious family member, Monroe made it over to where Roy stood in the shade of the peach tree, his forearms resting on the old rail fence.

"Monroe Scott." Monroe held out his hand and the older gentleman shook it. "I thought I'd take a moment to properly introduce myself and thank you for allowing me to crash the party."

"Roy Graham. Good to meet you, son, and of course you're welcome. If Tess wants you here, we want you here. I understand you're a firefighter?"

"Yes, sir." Monroe mimicked Roy's posture, taking in swaths of red and orange behind the mountains they faced. To the untrained eye, perhaps this sunset didn't look any different than usual, but Monroe knew the thick cloud capping the mountain range was smoke from the fires. And it would get closer and hazier every day until the fires were gone. "On a mission to save as much of this gorgeous land as I can."

"How noble of you." Sincerity soaked his words and genuine appreciation bracketed the almost teal-colored eyes he'd passed down the generations of Grahams for Tess to inherit. "We certainly thank you for it. We're kind of attached to this land."

Several moments of silence passed between them, both swathed in their appreciation of the land, before Roy spoke again. "Where are you from?"

"Eastern Idaho. I grew up in Spencer—that's where my family still is—but it's a little far from work. Right now, I have an apartment closer to our home base. It wouldn't take long to commute if they let me use the helicopter, but seeing as how they don't give me access to the ship and pilot whenever I want them, it took me a bit longer to drive here."

"You aren't heading home every night then?"

"No. We've been sleeping under the stars near base camp most nights, though tonight has sure made me miss family." Monroe turned toward the family fun going on behind them and leaned back against the fence. "They get together at least once a month doing pretty much the same thing." He watched Gary get tackled, ganged up on by two boys who looked to be about twelve, and laughed. "Mind if I ask you a question?" Monroe didn't bother to wait for permission. "As you might be aware, helitack firefighting runs four to five months of the year, so in addition to my job with the forest service, I also run a business reclaiming old wood and do a little construction on the side. I buy from farmers and ranchers mostly, but anyone who wants to get rid of old fences and barns. Basically, anyone who has a wooden structure that's falling down and would cost more to fix than rebuild. I help the owner get it off their property and pay a little something in the process. You wouldn't happen to have any contacts would you?" He shoved his hands in his pockets. Might as well quit beating around the bush. "Or do you know who owns that gorgeous old barn off of County Road 122? That is a reclaimer's dream."

Monroe allowed images of the barn and the surrounding property to silence him.

The man turned his whole body so he could stare at Monroe, nailing him with a particularly sharp squint. "What are you trying to pull on me? Did Tess put you up to asking me about my property? Because that's kind of a cock-eyed way of asking me about the place."

Now it was Monroe's turn to be confused. "Your place? That old barn is yours? The one that looks like it's been abandoned years ago?"

"Looks like it?" The man let out a dry laugh that

turned into a cough. "That's because it has been. We haven't had horses out there since Ava went to college—what was that, seven, eight years ago?"

"Does that mean you're willing to sell?" Monroe's heart pounded with the question. He was used to managing adrenaline with his job, so finding himself on the nervous side now was a surprise. Either it was because he wanted the property so bad, or he recognized that making deals with family—or near-family—was risky. Even if it was fake near-family.

"I know you said you were looking at buying wood, not property, but I can't imagine selling the one without the other." Roy was a smart negotiator. If Monroe had known he owned the place, he wouldn't have shown his cards so early.

But buying the property hadn't exactly been part of Monroe's plan. He hesitated. It was the best seasoned wood he'd seen in a long time, it was in great condition, and there was a lot of it. Either he could sell it for a big project—like a whole house remodel—or sell to several customers. Either way, it might be worth buying land he could then re-sell. And buying the land at the same time meant he had a place to store the wood. So far in his business, he'd only bought wood he had clients lined up for because he didn't have the storage space, but he didn't want to risk losing this wood. "I'm good with that, sir, if the price is right."

The older man pressed his lips together. He looked

hard across the horizon as if he could see the future. "Let me ask you one thing before we settle on a purchase price. Why would you look to buy property in Cobble Creek when your fiancée is bound and determined to leave the area?"

Tess wasn't planning on staying in Cobble Creek? Monroe looked around him at the picturesque scenery and then sought out the beautiful redhead. He found Tess chatting animatedly with her sister and some aunts and uncles. "She hasn't left yet."

"I'm just suggesting you might want to talk to her about it before you sign on the dotted line, but since she's the listing agent, I'm sure it'll come up." Roy nodded his head toward the pasture side of the fence, and Monroe followed his cue for the two of them to turn back to the pasture side of the fence again. "You ready to talk turkey?"

Chapter Eight

"You need to tell us about your boyfriend." Aunt Marlene nudged Tess with her elbow. "He's awfully cute."

"He's not—" Ava started to correct Marlene, and Tess scrambled to interrupt her.

"He's a"—at least Ava quit talking when Tess started—"wildland firefighter. He works on the helitack crew rappelling."

"Ooh! That sounds exciting." As thrilled as Aunt Marlene was, if she were twenty years younger and single, Tess might have been worried. "And dangerous." Tess followed Marlene's eyes to Monroe, not that her attention had left him for long since they'd arrived. She could admire his physique from afar all evening. In fact, it could easily become her newest hobby. One she would never tire of. This time, however, she found him talking to Grandpa Roy. At first, she was amused, maybe even proud to see it, because obviously Monroe had been the one to initiate contact, walking purposely over to talk to him, but why?

The barn.

"As I was saying," Ava's tone took on the timbre of one on the precipice of making a big announcement. It was rude, but Tess needed to interrupt her again—both to avoid the word engagement as well as to prevent Monroe and Grandpa from talking about the barn.

"I'm sorry, guys." Tess rubbed her temples. "I've got a major headache coming on, so I'm going to go." She turned to give Ava the first hug, effectively cutting their conversation off completely, and then hugging her aunts.

Tess strolled across the yard at the shortest tangent after making sure she wouldn't get tagged in the head with a Frisbee. She wasn't lying about her headache per se, though she might have oversold it just a titch. Either way, a Frisbee to the back of the head wouldn't do her any favors.

"Hi, Grandpa," she said when she got close enough to get his attention without yelling. She walked up to Monroe and threaded her hands through around his closest forearm. "I'm sorry to pull you away so quickly." *No, I'm not.* "But I'm getting a headache. Any way you could take me home, sweetie?" She looked up at him with her best adoring face and hoped he wouldn't bust up laughing because she would invariably join in. She was barely holding it back as it was.

Seeing a quirk in Monroe's lips, Tess turned her attention to her grandfather to keep from losing her composure. If she had such a headache, she needed to keep it together.

"Of course." Monroe took his arm from her hands and slipped it around her shoulders. Heat burned through her shirt at his touch. He drew her close to his side, and for a moment she forgot where she was, but then he dropped his arm, putting out his hand for Grandpa to shake. "Good to meet you, sir."

Generic enough. No mention of the property. She must have gotten there in time. Tess breathed a little easier.

"Bye, Gramps." She leaned in for her usual hug, but when she pulled back, he took a moment to look into her eyes and he smiled. He always saw her for who she was, and he liked her for it.

"You've got a good man here, darlin'. Don't let him go."

Tess stepped back, confused. This was spiraling out of control way too fast. How had she gotten here? She swallowed, trying to figure out what to say, but he said it for her.

"Now take her back and let her rest, son. We'll talk later."

Mornings were generally the best time at work. She needed those first few hours, before clients were available for tours, to pull comparisons, scour new listings, and print out specs, but today Tess was exhausted. If she took a quick power nap—ten minutes at the most—she'd be set for the rest of the day.

She tucked the throw pillow into the corner of her office love seat as she did after most long-run days. Any time the run was over eight or nine miles, the energy drained from the effort needed to be replaced before she could go on with her day. At eleven miles, this morning's run was her last long workday run. She'd been ramping down since the twenty-miler a few Saturdays ago.

Being a planner, Tess had started training for the marathon six months in advance of the Cobble Creek Hobble because the last thing she wanted to do was hobble her way across the finish line, and she was right on target. Tess had followed the training schedule religiously, her paces were right where she wanted them, and Ava or not, she was going to do great. Or so she told herself in her pep talk every day. Originally, her plan had been not to walk a step, but with her sister joining the race, the stakes had ratcheted up. Now she needed to keep a steady pace.

While her body was exhausted, Tess couldn't turn off her mind. After only a few moments on the couch, she sprang up, opting instead for a banana and some orange juice she'd brought with her. A glucose pick-me-up would be better than sleep anyway. She'd taken her first sip when her phone buzzed. It was a little early for business calls to start coming through.

The image of Grandpa Roy, his characteristic black Resistol perched on his full head of hair, with his white mustache and lopsided grin in front of Electric Peak filled her phone's screen. But why would Grandpa be calling her? Was he all right?

She hit the call-back button, panic thudding in her chest until she realized if something had happened, he would have called her father. Or, if it had been worse, he wouldn't have been calling, her father would. Maybe her blood sugar really was low for her to go off worrying about that kind of thing instead of remembering the obvious. Of course his call was about the listing.

Tess stared out the window as she waited for him to answer. Tree branches swayed in the breeze, back lit by a weak blue sky masked in a haze. Even still, it was predicted to be another extremely hot day.

"Sweet pea!" Grandpa finally answered. "You called back. I was leaving you a voice mail. Did you hear it?"

"Not yet. I figured it'd be better to chat instead. What's up?"

"Did you list my property?"

She'd known this was coming. After opening her email and seeing that the property had been denied historical status, Tess had no more excuses, so she actually was planning on listing today. "It's first on my list this morning."

"Whew! So you haven't yet." She could feel the relief in Grandpa's tone.

Maybe he changed his mind. She mirrored that relief.

"Well, you can mark it off your To-Do list."

"No problem." Tess allowed her joy to embellish her words.

"Next step, I guess, would be writing the contract, if you don't mind doing that for us. This way you still earn your commission, right, sweet pea? Unless, of course, you've already written it up?"

She must have missed something. "I'm sorry, Grandpa, what are you talking about?"

"The agreement your fiancé and I came to last night. I was sure the two of you had discussed it. I mean since the place will be yours after the two of you marry and all."

Tess's throat went dry and she took the lid off her water bottle in preparation for taking a big swig. She almost couldn't even breathe. Was Monroe taking advantage of their pretend engagement to cheat the old man from what was rightfully his? Would Grandpa even

THE COMBUSTIBLE ENGAGEMENT

have sold it to him if he hadn't thought they were engaged?

"Could you remind me the terms so I have everything right?"

"Eh, I'm a little fuzzy on the details now. I'm sure if you ask Monroe, he'll let you know."

I'm sure he will, the swine. "Thanks for letting me know. I'll take care of it."

"And you'll let me know when it's ready to sign?"

If it gets that far. "Will do."

Tess knew when she hung up that she should take a moment before contacting Monroe, and maybe that should have been more time than it took to dump half a ream of slick color fliers with the old barn printed on them into the trash can next to her desk. What a stinking waste of time and money.

Grandpa said you two came to an arrangement last night? Tess texted Monroe.

She navigated to the folder of paperwork and images on her computer, but she couldn't quite get herself to hit the delete button, no matter how much the hot-head part of her wanted to. She would need to make sure the new listing she'd been working on didn't get activated, but it was way too early to delete anything. Maybe the property wouldn't make it through escrow. Maybe this was all a misunderstanding.

Her phone rang. Monroe.

Tess considered not answering, but figured she was

as calm as she would ever be. If he wanted to do this voice-to-voice, fine by her. She swiped to answer.

"Before you say anything," Monroe said, "let me explain."

Oh, this better be good. "Okay." Tess said as flatly as she could manage.

"Your grandfather and I talked about a lot of things last night including the family, living in Cobble Creek, and life in general." He paused and Tess didn't respond. "He asked about my reclaiming business, and I told him. I asked if he knew of anyone who might be selling wood I could use, and he said he had some people he'd like to get me in touch with. A mutually beneficial relationship—his words, not mine. When I asked about the barn specifically, you know, asking if he knew who owned it, he told me." Again, he paused, and again Tess kept her silence, unwilling to absolve the guilt he was feeling. "The terms should be agreeable to you since I wouldn't let him negotiate. When I heard what he was asking, I insisted on paying him the full amount."

While she was relieved he didn't try to take advantage of their personal relationship—pretend or otherwise, it still didn't make sense.

"Do you normally pay that much for wood you plan to resell?"

"Of course not, but this includes the property. I assume you listed at fair market value."

With room to negotiate. "Of course. But why buy the whole thing if you aren't even sticking around?"

Tess heard a vehicle drive by in the background before Monroe spoke again. "It's an investment, Tess. I'm sure you've heard of those. After I sell off the barn wood, I can sell the plot of land separately. In fact, I'll even have you list it when I'm done with it. That way you'll make your commission twice."

When he was done with it? When he had used it up, dismantled it, and removed all of the unique charm and the memories and her childhood. This was most definitely not about commission.

She almost said, *Don't do me any favors*, until she realized she still needed him to. Was the sale of the barn worth losing Ava's respect and embarrassing herself within the whole family?

Tess couldn't bring herself to speak around the lump in her throat. She clenched her eyes tight and pinched the bridge of her nose to keep tears from forming. It was a piece of property. For a place she probably hadn't been in five years at least. And she didn't even plan on sticking around Cobble Creek herself. Why was she harassing him so much?

When she didn't answer, Monroe broke her reverie. "Can I ask a question?" His voice was so soft and humble, Tess's heart softened just a tiny bit. "Why does it matter so much? I mean, I realize it is your grandfather's property and as such likely holds sentimental value, but if I didn't buy it, someone else would."

The man had a good point. Silence stretched between them, a weight over the phone line.

"You're right." She let the weight fall. If anyone should feel used, it should be Monroe, and he didn't seem to be bothered by it. "What were the agreed-upon terms?" she asked meekly, pen poised to take notes.

Chapter Nine

"Guess what?" Monroe spoke to his fellow helitack crew members over the drone of the helicopter noise. Each member of the crew had their assignment, which included Monroe keeping his eyes peeled for the ten Standard Firefighting Orders and eighteen Watchout Situations, but they had a couple minutes to chat. "I'm going to be a property owner."

The helicopter soared over the blackened tree skeletons on the way to the drop point. For some reason, it reminded Monroe of his barn wood. Eventually this would be the site of forest renewal, but it would take years to get back to being thick and healthy again. Sometimes it was easier to distance himself emotionally from the death and destruction fire exacted on the landscape, but that was exactly why he did what he did every day trying to save it.

"You bought a house?" One of the younger crew members, Reggie, looked like he was being left out of the joke. "Here or back in Idaho?"

"You're talking that barn, aren't you?" Ryan remembered. Reggie, though, hadn't been with the others that day in Cobble Creek.

"Exactly." Monroe gathered the gear at his feet, knowing they were getting close. "I had to buy the land that barn's sitting on to get the wood, but it'll be worth it, I think. It's a prime piece of land, and it'll sell easily when I'm done with it. The barn, though . . ." Monroe allowed his words to trail off as he pictured what he could do with it. "It has the best gray wood out there—the perfect age for reclaimed wood projects. I've got tons of buyers who will pay top dollar. It's a gold mine." Monroe was pleased with the prospect, and talking to someone other than Tess about it was helping. It wasn't his fault she wasn't happy about the sale.

"But why?" Johnny said. "Buying wood, I understand. Buying property? Not so much. You have the money to invest in that?" Most people would be uncomfortable with such a personal financial question, but this was Johnny. Of course he asked. "Can you really sell that much wood? I wouldn't want to be responsible for trying to manage all of that from out of town. And then having to offload the property in the end?" He thumped Monroe on his helmet. "When do you have time to invest in finding buyers, preparing for shipping, all that other stuff, huh? You trying to find excuses to get away from us, man? We ain't got that kind of time away from the crew."

"Yeah, I know." Monroe shrugged. Johnny didn't give Monroe enough credit for the side business he'd built the past few years, but he was right that this took Monroe's reclaiming business up a-whole-nother level. "I like spending time with you guys, but maybe I don't want to be in this gig forever. I'm getting old."

"And slow," Johnny said.

"And tired," Ryan added.

"And you want to settle down. We get it," Reggie said.

Those guys. Johnny got it, Monroe knew. Johnny was only a year behind Monroe in experience, and after nearly a decade working the fires, well, Johnny could at least understand that nudge to move on to the next adventure. But Reggie? Monroe wanted to punch him. Young kid didn't have three years' worth of fires under his helmet to go all judgmental on his supervisor.

Besides, that wasn't what he was saying at all. They weren't even supposed to agree with him. "Maybe I wouldn't mind being in one place longer than six weeks at a time. Maybe I like the fact that there's enough wood to keep me busy for a while—all in one spot."

"But you love rappelling." Maybe Reggie wasn't so much trying to convince Monroe as much as trying to justify his own life choices.

Monroe ignored him.

"Are you going to hire someone to manage the property then when it's time to go on the next deployment?" Ryan leaned forward, putting his elbows on his knees.

That's what he'd done so far. "Wasn't planning to." Saying it out loud helped Monroe feel even better about the plan he was creating.

The men, however, just stared at him.

"I couldn't get him to sell just the wood." As if that explained everything—or even anything. Monroe fixed the strap on his helmet, ready for their landing. They had work to do. "Maybe I'd like to have a family of my own someday." Maybe even soon. He thought of cute little Lainey and the even younger toddlers at the Graham family get-together.

"Ha!" Johnny elbowed Ryan next to him. "I told you it was that girl." Johnny directed his gaze at Monroe again. "Did you see her again? That girl from the pharmacy?"

The question he'd been waiting for all night. "I did, actually, and she kind of asked me to marry her."

They whooped to Monroe's declaration at the same time the helicopter landed on the top of the highest peak, barely enough room for the crew to unload. It was time to cut the fires off from behind. Stop them from progressing this way before they snaked around to the other side of the mountain and that much closer to civilization. Monroe loved his job, that much was certain, but he wasn't averse to trying something new either, if he had the right motivation.

❁

THE CRUNCH of engine tires on gravel and a conversation pulled Monroe from the light sleep he'd fought for all night. It was still well before dawn of his day off, but Monroe couldn't take base camp one more second. After this many years as a wildland firefighter, he knew better than to spend the night at base if he didn't have to, but he'd been so exhausted when he returned from a full day of rappelling and delivering and rescuing the day before, he'd been sure he would drop off like a rock avalanche down a cliff, but no. No, he'd heard every footstep around camp, every slap of the portable restroom door, every intermittent conversation, and he couldn't take one more. He much preferred the nights when the crew was in the backcountry, away from base, where they would throw out tarps and sleeping bags under star-pricked black-domed nights, deep in the nature they were fighting hard to save. There was nothing better than camping in a safe zone, dining on MREs from their packs, away from the world—well, except maybe a real bed. Those rocked.

Monroe grabbed his things and crawled out of his tent. Lit by unrelenting light and accompanied by the constant hum of the generators that powered them,

Monroe made his escape. What he should have done last night was throw his sleeping bag into his pickup and drive out the Graham's barn. He'd been tempted to do just that, but a verbal agreement alone didn't reassure him Tess Graham wouldn't call the sheriff out to throw him off the property for different reasons this time.

But she wouldn't find him this early in the morning. If she did, he could claim he was taking another look—which was the truth. Not that it would change his mind about buying the property. He'd never been so certain of anything in his life. What it meant, though—what his next step would be and where this path would lead—now that was still a mystery to him.

By the time Monroe's pickup turned off the old county road and bounced down the dusty lane through the trees, the sun was just starting to filter through the haze of drifting smoke. The smoke was thinner here than at base camp for sure, but he knew it was there, obscuring what would have been a bright blue summer sky any other year.

He parked and rolled down his windows, allowing the silence to settle around him like the dust he'd stirred up. The barn loomed above him, a majestic structure that would be a shame to lose, honestly. What if he didn't tear it down? With fresh perspective, Monroe inspected it again. It probably wouldn't take much to stabilize the structure and make it into his warehouse.

He'd have a home base for his business and Tess could send him more remodeling clients like Lauren and David—if she ever let go of her anger at his buying the property. But then again, if he saved the barn, would that be enough to assuage her animosity?

With his mind full of possibilities and the logistics of the change in plans, he grabbed a camp chair from the bed of his pickup and slung it over his shoulder. Walking the perimeter of the grounds, he made plans and mental lists until he made it to the cheerful creek winding through some tall cottonwoods. Wider troughs cut from the sandstone proved that when swollen with spring run-off, the stream could be much more violent than the bubbles skipping across the worn rocks. No matter the season, this was easily his favorite spot on the property.

Monroe set up his chair at a gentle bend in the brook, exhaustion flowing around him effortlessly. After removing his shoes, he plunged his feet into the water, bracing himself for the refreshing, but almost icy cold. To balance the coolness, Monroe leaned back in the chair, soaking up the warmth of the sun on his face, not even fighting to keep his eyes open. The whisper of the wind in the trees, the song of the meadowlarks, and the trickle of the water combined into the best lullaby he could imagine. The place was paradise.

When his phone rang, he couldn't remember where he was, but to be honest, he was used to that feeling.

Groping his jacket pocket for the phone, he allowed the sights to settle back in, reminding him, but at the same time, making calculations of how long it would take him to get to the helipad if he were getting called in.

He didn't bother to look at the ID. "Monroe here."

"Hi." The hesitation afterward had him scrambling to place the voice in his sleep-induced fog. "Would you be able to swing by my office to sign the paperwork on the property today?"

Oh, Tess.

He snapped fully awake. *Tess.* Her words were clipped, and she wasn't trying to disguise her contempt.

"Okay." He kept his voice neutral, though it still made no sense to him why she was so upset. If he hadn't bought the place someone else would have.

Roy Graham was more than determined to unload the property. There couldn't have been a more motivated seller. In fact, as soon as he signed the papers and his cash went through, the whole sale would be finished within days, if he was understanding it correctly.

The other thing that didn't make sense about this whole situation, though, was why it bothered *him* so much that Tess was mad. It wasn't like they had much history or even that he knew her well, but somehow he needed to get on her good side again. A thought occurred to him. "What's your schedule like today? I think we should look at houses."

"What on earth for?"

He could almost see the wrinkled-brow confusion on her face, and he felt satisfaction that he'd caught her off guard. First step through the door. "I mean, if we're engaged, I should at least look like I'm moving here, right?"

"I don't know." At least she was considering it. "But I'm not taking you to any occupied homes. It wouldn't be fair to the seller to get their hopes up with someone who's not really interested."

That she hated giving in to him gave him a satisfied pleasure. He would change her mind about him. She needed him, which was why she was still talking to him, but he wanted her to want him around as well.

"Totally understandable." Monroe turned on the speaker and set the phone in his lap. With his discarded hoodie, he dried off his feet and pulled on his socks.

"Lucky for you, I do have some homes I was going to preview for clients today, so I suppose you could tag along."

He would be happy to do so, as long as he could get the happy Tess back. But he was up for the challenge. In fact, it made trying all the more interesting. "Text me a time and an address, and I'll meet you there."

"Fine." It sounded like she was anything but fine with it, but he'd take her at her word.

Monroe knew he was teetering on the brink of feeling Tess's wrath. While it was fun to tease her, he was playing with fire. And he had enough experience with fire to know, you didn't mess with it.

You could use it to your advantage, though. He'd set more than enough fires of his own—the whole fighting fire with fire scenario. But now wasn't the time for that. He needed to cool things down if he wanted any kind of relationship with Tess to progress without burning out. What could he do to smooth things over?

It wasn't until he was driving down Main Street and saw the striped awning of Graham's Pharmacy that the idea struck him. Finding a parking spot that wasn't reserved for the handicapped, Monroe parked his truck, hoping Tess's father would be in a friendly mood. He needed to make things right with the man or this pseudo-relationship would end up burnt to a crisp before it even got started.

Monroe tracked Gordon down at the pharmacy counter.

"Good morning, Monroe." The way Gordon looked through the tops of his cheaters at Monroe, he felt like he was staring down a bear.

"Sir, it seems you and I need to have a talk." Monroe tried to find that delicate balance between contrition and confidence. He walked up to the pharmacy counter and stuck out his hand. "I'm sorry I didn't take the opportunity to introduce myself before this."

Monroe searched his memory for the words actually said Tess's father's presence when he'd come in with his crewmen. How bad had it gotten? He tried not to cringe. If he remembered right, he'd tried to stand up for Tess. That was how he hoped Gordon would remember it too. He just hoped the fact that they hadn't acted like they'd known one another didn't cause too many problems.

Gordon accepted the handshake. "It seems we do." Dressed in a white pharmacist's coat, his light-blue collared shirt and red tie underneath, Gordon looked a lot more professional than he had mixing up sodas at the fountain.

"I know I'm doing all of this backward. Tess and I, well, we kind of decided on the spur of the moment. I'm sure you can understand—she's one special woman." Everything he was saying was true.

Gordon stared him down. "She's never been that impulsive before."

Monroe shook his head as if he completely understood. "Me neither, you have to believe me. I guess Tess and I just bring that out in each other." Monroe sighed. "I'm sure you noticed we're still working on the ring. Well, that's not the only thing. Before I give her one, I plan to sit down with you and your wife to ask for her hand. But before I can do that, I guess, well, I need to allow you to get to know me. And to allow you to get to know me, well, I was hoping you could help me out. I need—" He ran a hand over the back of his neck. "—Tess's favorite soda flavor."

Gordon breathed out a laugh. "After that intro, how

can I refuse? Just let me give you a little advice first. You may have rushed into this engagement, but please don't rush into the marriage. I appreciate that you're trying to make up for it now. I get the impulsive, overpowering, all-commanding feeling of love. Just don't let it overtake your good sense." His piercing teal eyes, an older version of Tess's, bore into him.

"Yes, sir." If the man only knew.

Monroe actually felt bad about that. He could like this man.

Gordon relaxed his shoulders, and Monroe knew the lecture was through. "About the soda flavor. Unfortunately, son, there isn't an easy answer to that question. It depends on how much you ticked her off. Is this an 'I was thinking about you and I wanted to do something nice' or is this more of an 'I'm a jerk, and I hope you can forgive me'?"

"I'm hoping it's somewhere in between." Monroe ran a hand over the back of his neck. "Wow. Am I really that transparent?" At least the man was having a nice laugh at his discomfort.

Gordon leaned his elbows on the counter. His eyes gave the impression of having x-ray vision, and Monroe tried not to squirm. He hadn't technically done anything wrong—unless you counted the whole lying to the man about being engaged to his daughter deal. Monroe shifted his weight, but didn't look away.

Grant shook his head as only an indulgent father

can. "Tess is a complicated one. Her tastes change fairly frequently, which means you probably can't go wrong with just about anything, but that also makes it impossible to know what her favorite of the moment is. In this case, I'm thinking you should ask Preston to whip up a phosphate with chipped ice, pineapple, and orange juice." Monroe panicked he might not be able to remember that. Didn't it have some fancy name with a cow in it? But Gordon was still talking. "Not too terribly sweet for mid-morning, since it's too early for ice cream right?"

Monroe faked being taken aback. "It's never too early for ice cream."

Gordon laughed. "I have to say I agree with you there, but since Tess is training for the marathon, I figure something fruity with a bit of a kick to get her moving, and yet sweet enough to get on her good side."

The concept of a soda flavor saying all that, having that much influence, was foreign and exciting. But hey, if it worked, so much the better.

Monroe had to concede the point. "Sound advice. Thank you, sir." Monroe turned to leave, wondering what he should be saying to his fake future father-in-law that he hadn't even considered. "I hope someday to know her as well as you do."

"Looks like you're well on your way."

Monroe sauntered up to the soda counter and

ordered the drink for Tess as well as a plain orange juice for himself and turned to head out.

In the meantime, Gordon had walked to the front of the store. "May the force be with you and the odds forever in your favor," Gordon said as Monroe pushed the door open with his hip. Monroe lifted a Styrofoam cup in salute. "And let me know how well the orange pineapple worked."

"Will do," Monroe said. "And thank you." Monroe could really come to like this man who welcomed him in so easily. "See you later."

The clock on Monroe's pickup dash warned he would be cutting it close, but hopefully his peace offering would make up for it.

It was a good thing he recognized Tess's Honda when he pulled up to the house the GPS led him to, or Monroe wouldn't have thought he was in the right place. He pulled to the curb behind her SUV on a quiet, perfect street. Established oaks and sycamores shaded wide sidewalks, and the houses were set back as if giving passersby a polite, wide berth. The home was a palatial colonial. Way more house than he could see himself ever needing, but especially while he was single.

"Big house," he said, the only thing he could think of that was neutral. He handed her the drink and took a sip of his own before leaning back into his truck to set it back into the cup holder.

"Not your style?" She was observant. "Good thing

THE COMBUSTIBLE ENGAGEMENT

it's for one of my clients, then, and not you." Monroe heard the subtext loud and clear—she was choosing homes for people actually paying commission instead of wasting her time. Well, that was fine. "Come on." She nodded with her head. Without even asking what she was going to be drinking, Tess took a sip of her drink, her eyelids fluttering closed in appreciation. "*Mmm.* This really hits the spot."

She lifted her chin and swallowed slowly as if appeasing a chaffed throat. The EMT in him finally woke up.

"Sore throat?"

She nodded and relished another sip.

"Your eyes—" Monroe stepped close enough he could hear each breath as they stood face to face. At no more than a few inches shorter than he was, she was the perfect height. A subliminal way of showing she was his equal in every way. Her teal eyes looked bluer when bracketed with fine, red lines. "They're bloodshot. Running and smoky air aren't a good combo."

Tess stepped back and turned on her heel, lifting her fob to lock her Honda. "It's nothing. Allergies. I get them every summer."

"Okay." There wasn't anything he could do other than to back off and let her make her own choices. It wasn't worth ruining the day over.

Tess looked over the cup at him with a raised eyebrow, and he couldn't remember a cuter expression on any woman. She was challenging him to push the air-quality issue, but he wasn't going to.

"It really is good." She took another long drink and then smiled slowly. "Might even be my new favorite."

Was her rigid demeanor softening up just a smidge? He'd give Gordon a fist bump right about now, if he could.

A flicker of her smile warmed Monroe from the inside. Observing her appreciate something as minor as a few flavors swirling around in carbonation made him feel grateful for the small things. "I can't believe you just tried it, without even asking the flavor." He paused a beat. "Nice to know you trust me so well."

She smirked at him. "I saw the Graham's Pharmacy logo. Anything from them is good."

"Wow, that's not biased at all," he teased.

"It's not bias, it's experience."

She led him up the sidewalk between lines of mature box hedges cut in strict rectangles. A pair of massive columns stood sentry, guarding a heavy walnut door flanked by sidelights.

"There isn't *anything* from Graham's you don't like?" Monroe gave her a dubious look. "Don't worry," he whispered, "I won't tell anyone. It'll be our little secret."

"We have got a few of those—secrets—don't we?" she whispered back conspiratorially, leaning toward him. She stood straight, then, and returned her voice to her normal volume. "I can't think of anything I've tried from them I didn't like, though some can be a little on the sweet side—like a drinkable dessert. Those are special-occasion only."

Her father knew her well.

Monroe and Tess stepped into a large, so-formal-it-was-stuffy foyer with gleaming hardwoods and rooms blossoming on either side of them. A fussy chandelier dripped down from the high ceiling on one side and a heavily molded fireplace and mantle dominated the room on the other. Monroe thought he would suffocate if he'd have to live in such a place, but he could walk through if she needed to.

"Speaking of taste, is this yours?" He wanted to gauge her reaction before blowing it with his own. And if he could get her talking about herself, maybe she wouldn't ask him.

"Eh." Tess was noncommittal. "I like the high ceilings—I mean, they're better than, say, a ranch with eight-footers, but I'm kind of a higher-the-better gal."

Their footsteps echoed through the room as they walked through, taking no more time than it took to get the layout, though he had a feeling she was taking note of more details than he noticed.

"And wood floors. Those seem to be what everyone wants now, right, rather than carpeting, right?" Not that he cared much.

"Definitely. A lot of people are grossed out by carpet, but I just try not to think about it much. I mean, what's the difference between steam-cleaning carpet versus non-porous floors that probably have barely been mopped? But old carpet is just plain nasty." She opened the master closet and took a peek, but then closed it again. "There I go playing devil's advocate again. Personally, I like a wood floor too, but maybe not one so glossy, you know, but not rustic either. Natural, somehow."

The woman was confusing.

"You know who would like this house, though? Ava."

Her twin.

"I thought you said she was a barrel racer." He watched as she trailed her fingers down the stair railing. She had grace and charm. A deadly combination.

"Yes. She's also finishing med school and likes to frequent art museums. People rarely fit into the tiny little boxes others like to shove them into."

"Good point." He walked alongside her but crossed his arms over his chest. "What kind of box do you have me shoved into?"

She stopped to look at him, her head cocked and her eyes narrowed. "I just told you I don't do that."

"But if you did . . ." He left it hanging, waiting for her to answer, but still she paused. "Isn't that part of your job? Reading people so you know what kinds of houses will speak to them, even if they don't know themselves?"

THE COMBUSTIBLE ENGAGEMENT

"All right, yes. Let's see . . . Reclaimed wood. That would indicate to me that you like old things. Yet firefighter always says something a little more modern to me." She tapped her index finger on the railing. "I'm going to go out on a limb here and say you like modern—clean lines, minimal, yet you like to rough it up with a little rotten wood?"

He tried to keep from laughing, but it didn't exactly work. He shook his head at her. "*Rotten wood.* Only rotten souls would think of it as rotten wood." He bumped her shoulder with his and she chuckled.

"Fine. Maybe not rotten. How about *old*?"

"Aged," he corrected.

She stepped down into the foyer again. "Decrepit."

"Distinguished."

"Worn out," she countered.

"Experienced."

"I'm not sure experienced is actually a good thing in this context. Remember the carpet conversation? I say it ranks up there with obsolete and outdated."

Monroe sucked in his cheeks to keep from cracking a smile. "Seasoned, time-honored, tried and true."

"Because you just can't trust newly milled wood." She closed the front door behind them and tugged on it to make sure it was secured.

She thought she was so clever. Well, maybe she was. "Exactly. It will warp and split. Green wood is very bad." Monroe tried to sound like this was a serious conversation rather than the flirty banter it was turning into.

"Ha. The only thing I know about green wood is that it doesn't burn—which should be a good thing in your mind. I mean, what kind of firefighter collects scrap wood that would probably fuel any wildland fire faster than the forest itself?"

"Which is exactly why I like to reuse it—put it into something useful where it will be protected—instead of leaving it out to catch fire."

They reached the curb and Tess stopped at her SUV. "Want to ride with me? We can come back for your truck later."

With a silent nod, Monroe deposited his keys back into his pocket. He barely held back the quip about women drivers he'd been about to make. Spending so much time with firefighters and away from normal society could cause some problems if he wasn't careful. It would only have been a joke, of course, but Tess didn't know him well enough to know that, and his mom would have been disappointed.

He submissively climbed into Tess's SUV, secretly happy to lean back and enjoy someone else driving for a change. In fact, it was kind of nice, spending easy time with Tess without having to make decisions about where to go or what to do.

The next house they stopped in front of was completely different from the first. This one clearly was built in the '70s. Diagonal boards ran down either side of the front door. Honestly, it was a mess. The evergreen shrubs were severely overgrown, blocking many of the home's aluminum windows, and weeds had long since overtaken what might have once been a yard.

Things got worse when Tess opened the door. "Holy dark wood Batman."

Did she really just say that? Monroe laughed. "You did say you like hardwood floors."

"Floors. Not floors that extend onto all the walls. I feel like I'm in a cave." Tess flicked on the light, but the single amber-shaded lamp hung from a chain in the entry didn't help much. "And who puts this kind of a lamp in the foyer anyway?"

Exactly. Especially with no furnishings of any sort to dilute the attention from the sorry light.

Monroe closed the door behind them. "Out of curiosity, is this how you always show houses?"

"Of course not." Tess looked at him like he was crazy, but she was the one who was making fun of everything about the house.

"Okay. If I'm understanding your subtle hints, you're not so much a fan of this wood. How about slathered white?"

"The paneling?" She grimaced at the paneling, and he was glad it didn't have any feelings. "I guess it would be better. More buyers prefer the cottage look when paneling is painted, but I'm more of an exposed-brick kind of gal." She walked over to a built-in bookcase. "But this." She ran her hand along the shelves, clearly in awe. "I'm a completely sucker for bookcases of any sort. Someday, my dream home will have a library."

He raised his eyebrows at her. "How very old-fashioned of you in this digital age. I'm intrigued by you. Don't you read ebooks?"

"I read books," Tess emphasized. "In every form. Paperback, hardback, ebook, audio. I'm even known to watch them as movies on occasion."

"That sounds dangerous." They walked into the sorriest excuse for a kitchen he'd seen in a long time, not that that was saying much. Monroe was sure Tess saw more homes in one day than he'd seen in a lifetime.

"Oh, it is definitely dangerous." Tess absently opened a few of the old, empty cabinets and allowed them to bang closed. "You know most of the time the movies are nowhere as good as the book." She headed into the next room without even a comment about the chipped laminate counter tops with the black-ribbed rubber edge. What was that? In case you wanted to play bumper cars in the house?

They went through a narrow set of double doors what would be the formal dining room. He practically gave himself a concussion on the low-hanging chandelier without a table to warn them.

"Aside from the gaudy glass chandelier that you

THE COMBUSTIBLE ENGAGEMENT

might have ruined anyway—" She smirked at him. "This is a fantastic room."

He rubbed his head where he hit it. "You're worried about the light fixture and not me?"

Tess opened her mouth to make what was sure to be some flippant remark but then closed it again, looking repentant. "Are you okay?"

She didn't mean it, and he didn't need her to. He was fine.

"*Anyway*," she emphasized, "I would make this into the library. It's far enough away from the living room to be quiet and away from anyone watching TV. It's got great light." She walked to the window and pulled back the thick burlap curtain. If the cobwebby shrub crowding the glass were cut back, Monroe could tell she would be right. "The kitchen can easily accommodate a large family dining table, so I wouldn't have another here." She pointed things out as she circled the room. "Some built-ins there. Ooh, one of those library ladders—"

"A library ladder, really?" Monroe chuckled. "Because you can't reach the top of an eight-foot bookshelf?"

"Okay, so this house isn't my ideal." She dismissed him, going back to her fantasy. "A couple of comfy chairs..."

She turned around, her eyes glassy, and Monroe could tell she was picturing her dream home. Given the things she'd mentioned so far, could he come up with a house that she would love? Maybe if he kept pumping her for details.

She chuckled to herself. "Ava and I used to do this thing . . . See my mom was pretty busy working shifts at the pharmacy and the closest library at the time was in Duckdale Hollow, which can be a drive, so she'd only take us to the library once a week. Ava and I would check out the maximum allotment of titles, stuffing our bags with books—and let me tell you, as the summers progressed, it got harder and harder to find books we hadn't read before. Anyway, Ava and I would sit in the living room reading our books for hours. As soon as one of us finished one, we'd close it with a snap and announce, 'Good book.' And then dig out another one." Tess looked up to the ceiling, remembering with a smile. "Leave it to Ava to make reading into a competition. It was no longer about the joy of reading, it was about who finished the most books in a week—or at least that seemed to be the unspoken goal. We never got so serious we didn't find time to play outside or go riding or whatever, and I never lost my appetite for reading, but it's kind of funny looking back. We must have been odd kids."

Monroe soaked in the memory as if it were his own. And it could have been if you substituted books for Pokémon cards or Mario Kart. He missed his own sister.

"Sounds like the two of you have a really good relationship."

"We did." Tess's words felt stony now as she walked him through the French doors back into the entry way. The house had been a donut, and Monroe hadn't even realized they'd made it all the way through already.

Obviously, he'd said the wrong thing. Should he push for more details, encourage her to fix it, or butt out? "But . . ." he trailed off so Tess could explain if she wanted to.

"In high school and when she went away to college, I was jealous and competitive and allowed little wedges to break us apart." She shook her head at herself, her hand on the doorknob. "I need to fix that." Her sad eyes were sincere. "While I wish she hadn't brought Glenn with her, being with Ava these last couple of days has made me realize I want to do better. I want that relationship back."

Lying to her sister about being engaged probably wouldn't help with the sisterly trust, but now probably wasn't the best time to bring that up.

"I couldn't think of a more deserving relationship to rescue." He clapped his hand on her shoulder, just as he would have with one of his crew mates, but touching her, even though the softness of her blouse, felt anything but friendly. He allowed his hand to slide over her scapula and linger a moment, but not enough to be creepy. He hoped. "Ready for the next house?"

Tess opened the door, and they left behind the emptiness of someone else's past. "What kind of house do you want to see?" She unlocked her SUV with the fob and they climbed in while he thought about it. "What's your ideal home?"

"My ideal home would have to be outside of town, for sure. Surrounded by trees or open land. That's probably highest on my list. Anything else I can deal with."

"Any . . . thing else?" She dragged it out as if he'd challenged her.

He was up for that challenge. "Hit me with your best shot. I bet I could make anything work."

"Oh, you are so on." Tess laughed wickedly, and Monroe knew he would not be able to get enough of this intriguing woman.

Chapter Ten

That morning, Monroe and his crew were flown in to get control of a new leg of the fire. Flames had jumped fire break cut in by hotshots a few days before, and now his crew had to dig a new line. No matter if they were wielding a chainsaw, McLeod rake, or Pulaski axe, or good old trusty shovel, after the hours they put in pounding at the roots and hard ground to clear a five-foot fire break, by noon, each crew member had earned his break. Not caring that they were covered in soot, sweat, and dirt, they were sprawled out rehydrating and filling the hole in their stomachs.

"You're telling me you spent five hours straight looking at houses neither one of you wants to buy? That sounds like absolute torture to me." Johnny shoved the last bite of his MRE into his mouth and kept talking. "Couldn't pay me enough to waste my day off like that."

Johnny probably wasn't even tasting his food, but then again, this type of food wasn't meant to be enjoyed. It was strictly for survival. Monroe took a bite of his own. It was okay and indicative of the day he'd spent in hard, satisfying work with a group of guys who he trusted with his life, literally, every single day. But what would it be like if he had someone like Tess at home, having dinners together like a normal couple? Even if one of them burned the dinner, it wouldn't actually taste like ash.

The guy could complain all he wanted, but nothing would make Monroe regret how he'd spent the previous day. It had been just about perfect in his estimation. He checked that he had all of his equipment secured one last time. "You guys ready? Let's do this."

They'd successfully gotten the area under control. What was left of this leg of the fire should burn itself out in the next few hours, so they'd radioed for pick-up and decided to catch a bite to eat while they waited for their ship to return. This was by far the best kind of day —they'd been able to keep last night's lightning strike from becoming a full-blown incident without the help of having to call in the engines or hotshots. Monroe wished that were always the outcome.

"You just want to get home to that pretty little lady." Ryan wiggled his eyebrows at Monroe.

"Can you blame me?" Monroe joked back, but he didn't have any plans to go see Tess that night which was probably good because the day was still young. Chances were the crew would be called out for three or four more jobs before the shift was done. "Speaking of days off and making an extra buck, I've been thinking about that barn I bought. I've got a new plan, but I need to hire a crew of reliable workers. Anyone know some guys up for the task?"

Ever since the house-hunting trip, Monroe couldn't scrub his mind of Tess. Tess and her opinions. She opened up to him like no other woman ever had—but not in a clingy way.

At first when he'd met Tess, he'd seen her as this hard, self-sufficient woman who had no compunction over asking for favors or taking exactly what she needed. Monroe had no worries that their fake engagement would hurt her in any way. She was a wildfire that could take over anything she set her mind to. He was perfectly happy to be the deadwood consumed by that fire and left behind when she had no more need for him —not because he didn't have the self-respect to protect himself, but precisely because he knew he could bounce back, and maybe even be better for the experience. If nothing else, this sham of an engagement would pass the time.

What he hadn't expected was for Tess to pull him in so completely, and give herself in return. She'd let him into her world, introduced him to her family, confided her favorite childhood memories, and even shared a few of her regrets and dreams. He was getting to know her. She was no longer this natural disaster waiting to happen, no longer a force to be reckoned with. But unfortunately, it wouldn't, couldn't, last. The way things were going with the fire, he could see his crew getting called back closer to home at any time.

But that barn. He needed to rip it down so he could harvest the wood and get the property ready to sell again. It was the best way to reclaim his money and close up loose ends before he was called back home. Still, the more Monroe got to know Tess, the more he realized how connected she was to that barn. He wasn't willing to relinquish the property to her, but maybe it wasn't time to tear it down. Yet.

"What do you have in mind?" Johnny was always ready to collect an extra buck.

"That old barn?" Monroe asked.

"The one falling down?" Johnny noticed H-8CM flying in on the horizon and stood, brushing off the back of his pants, and Monroe had to force himself not to laugh. As if they weren't all so filthy anyone would care what the man had sat in.

"I think we could save it. Reinforce the structure and make it into my warehouse. It's got some great storage potential, plenty of room to bring in what I'm harvesting elsewhere." His ideas spilled out one after another, gushing like an oil spill and pulsing forth until it was all out and irretrievable. The guys didn't need to know the specifics of what he planned to do—they didn't have a clue how big his reclaiming business had gotten over the past year.

Monroe cleared his throat against the thick, smoky air. "If I get my hands on the right tools and supplies, we could get the place solid in no time. You in?"

"If you're paying, it works for me," Johnny said.

❀

Sorry about your race, Monroe texted Tess the day before the Cobble Creek Hobble would have been held.

Monroe had been on duty sixteen-hour shifts since the house-hunting trip a few days back, but the last he knew, Tess had still been pushing herself to train despite the smoke-infused air. It was worse than doing yoga in an incense shop, and just as counter-productive. He'd tried to convince her to stop for her health, but when she hadn't accepted his advice, he understood. Abandoning a big goal like that, especially when it was right there within reach, would have been impossible for him as well.

He cringed at the hypocrisy of his advice. Working on the line breathing in the thick smoke completely unfiltered—Monroe didn't even want to think about the damage he was doing to his lungs. He'd developed a tolerance over the years, but didn't mean Tess should.

You heard about it then? she responded.

Yes. Stinks. I know you worked hard. He'd heard his supervisor had called Cobble Creek's mayor and sheriff to convince them to call it off, and knew that Tess had to be disappointed. Cancellation due to poor air quality was the only prudent course of action for the runners' health, but that didn't mean it sucked. He sent another text before she could respond. Alternative date instead?

He stared at his screen wondering if he should have been less vague, but this way, if she turned him down, he had plausible deniability.

Are you asking me out? she texted back without delay. That fact made him smile. Apparently, she wouldn't be opposed to such an idea.

If I don't get called in to work. He sent the text, but then added a quick follow-up. We need to be seen together, don't we? And since your day's plans fell through . . .

All week they'd been exchanging random texts. He hadn't had that kind of relationship with a woman for years. It started with Tess sending pictures of crazy wallpaper and horrible paint combinations and other laughable design choices. The next day she sent taunting photos of mouth-watering root beer floats, and he retaliated with severed rattlesnake tails and group pictures of him sliding down his rappelling rope.

He enjoyed their easy-going banter so much, he wasn't about to point out that texts weren't strictly necessary to pull off a fake engagement. No one but the two of them even saw the messages.

But it did help in getting to know her better.

WHAT DID YOU HAVE IN MIND?

WHY? WOULD YOU SAY NO? He wished he could see her expression to determine if she was going along with it as part of the fake engagement or if she was actually interested in spending time with him.

MAYBE.

He chuckled to himself. SURPRISE. YOU IN OR NOT?

I'M IN.

⁂

OF COURSE, the biggest reason Monroe didn't tell Tess any specifics about their date, besides not knowing if he'd actually be able to make it, was that he had no idea what to do. There were so many outdoor things he wanted to do with Yellowstone, the Grand Tetons, and Jackson all within a short drive's distance, but with the air quality being the reason for the change in her plans, it didn't seem fair to have her exercising outside in other activities.

DRESS FOR THE DATE? she texted Saturday morning after they'd arranged for him to pick her up at one.

IF YOU WANT, he texted back, unable to stop himself. He grinned, waiting for her reply.

Does that mean you'll be in a suit? Ha. Leave it to her to twist his meaning to suit her tastes.

My armor is at the blacksmith's. I'll be in jeans. Remember, I'm living out of a duffel bag. And everything in it was wrinkled and smelled like smoke. He lifted his nicest shirt to his nose. It passed the sniff test. And he had cologne.

Still not helpful. What will we be doing?

Don't ask questions around Christmas. Monroe toggled over to the internet app on his phone to find out if there was a florist in Cobble Creek. Did Tess like flowers? Or was there something better? He'd already done the soda thing...

It's August. Smarty pants.

Oh, right. Don't ask questions, school's out for the summer.

Not for much longer.

Doesn't matter. Still not answering questions. He'd considered a book instead of flowers, but considering his date idea, it wouldn't exactly work.

Ugh. You are no help at all. I'll make you sorry you didn't answer.

Oh, now that could be interesting. He'd love to know what she was thinking. Ha ha. How do you expect to do that?

No questions at this time. Oh, she was quick.

Or you'll refer me to your lawyer?

Exactly.

Monroe didn't know how to respond to that. He ought to break down and answer her question. After all, it made sense to clue her in on the day's plans so she could dress appropriately, but now she had him hooked. How exactly would she make him sorry he didn't tell her?

Pick you up after lunch. One o'clock. Monroe hit send, worrying he'd regret not giving in, but he didn't have much more time to invest thinking about it. Only being in Cobble Creek a couple of days a week made getting everything done on the barn a challenge. Especially when he was fighting exhaustion pretty much all the time. While the forest service couldn't work him more than sixteen hours a stretch, those were long days for anyone, especially when adding in carrying a one hundred-twenty-pound pack while rappelling from a hovering helicopter and navigating some of the steepest and most rugged terrain in the area.

For now, he had a meeting with the Steger brothers—a suggestion from Sheriff Trent Lockheart. Despite their interesting meeting when Tess made the trespassing call, Trent had become someone Monroe could enjoying hanging out with. After their air-quality meeting, Monroe started explaining about his reclaimed wood business. As soon as Trent heard about it, he dragged Monroe over to his place for dinner so he could show off the rustic remodel the Steger brothers had completed for him.

The Steger company truck broke through the trees, and Monroe switched mental gears from Tess to the property. Monroe and his crew had plans to reinforce the barn, but lately his brain starting tumbling about other ideas. His plans for the structure may just have evolved again, depending on the news the construction gurus gave him today.

"Welcome." Monroe stepped forward to shake hands with the two brothers who stepped out of the pickup. "Thank you so much for coming out."

"Of course." The older one, Seth, introduced both himself and his younger brother Jon. "Trent said you had some ideas and wanted to run them by someone."

Walking around his barn, throwing out ideas and finding they actually had merit, left Monroe as exhilarated as he'd been his very first rappel from a helicopter. As they inspected the structure from foundation to shingles and everything in between, all three of them were energized with possibilities. Monroe got so wrapped up in the what-ifs, plans, and sketches, he was surprised when Jon interrupted their session. "Hey, I hate to say it, but I'm supposed to meet my girlfriend in town for lunch."

Monroe checked the time on his phone. "Shoot! Is that the time?" He started walking the brothers to the barn door. "I've got a date too." One he certainly couldn't afford to be late to. At least he had a sandwich packed in his truck.

"We'll run some numbers and get back to you," Seth said. "That way you can have a better idea if it's worth proceeding."

Monroe clapped Seth on the back. "I really appreciate you taking the time to consult with me. I sure hope I didn't waste your time."

Seth laughed. "Talking construction—especially on ideas as fun as this—is never a waste of our time."

"It sounds like a really fun project," Jon said, opening the passenger door on their truck. "We'll be in touch."

❀

When Monroe knocked on Tess's Craftsman door, he braced himself for what he might see when she answered, but she opened the door showing off her running tan and toned muscles wearing a casual summer skirt, blouse, and wedge sandals—perfect for just about any occasion, except maybe hiking. Good thing he'd crossed that off that list.

"You look beautiful." Nervously, he shoved his hands in his pockets. "After that threatening text, I fully expected you'd either be wearing pajamas or formal wear." Almost too late, he realized how that might be interpreted. "Not that you wouldn't look just as beautiful in either of those outfits as well."

"Stop now," she shook her head warningly, "before

you hurt someone." She nudged him with her shoulder and then reached around him to grab her purse off the entry table. "Are we ready?"

He had the day off from work, an invigorating project percolating in his head, and a gorgeous redhead by his side. Yes, he was ready for anything. He just hoped he wouldn't blow it with the date he had planned.

"Are you okay in my truck?" Monroe looked at her skirt and high-heels dubiously. Although he had no personal experience wearing either, his sister complained plenty if she had to get into his truck dressed that way.

"What—and risk only finding handicapped parking?" She pulled a face. "I don't know if it's worth the risk."

"I'm never going to live that one down, am I?" Monroe grumbled good-naturedly. If the city would repaint and make sure their signs were visible . . .

Tess walked over to the passenger side of his pickup in what he was a decided was an answer. With outstretched hand, he helped her up the huge step and into her seat. The smile and appreciative look he received made him appreciate that she found him worth the time to tease.

Chapter Eleven

When Monroe didn't take the highway toward Duckdale Hollow, Tess tried to convince herself the date would still turn out all right, but she was skeptical. Having lived in Cobble Creek her whole life, Tess knew there wasn't much to do that she hadn't done before, but she tried to remind herself it was all new to Monroe.

Knowing Cobble Creek as well as she did, it only took a few minutes for Tess to guess where they were headed, though it didn't make much sense, really. When Monroe pulled into the parking lot of the public library, she knew she'd surmised correctly, yet figuring exactly what he had planned left Tess at a loss. A library? Was he researching something? Under the expectation of silence, they'd barely be able to speak to each other.

Still, the library. Was this because of the story she'd

shared with him? Her heart pounded as he helped her from the pickup by taking her hand. Then, without dropping it, he interlaced their fingers and guided her up the several steps to the front doors. "Is this okay?"

Never before had she heard this big, muscly outdoorsman sound hesitant. It was endearing to know he didn't always have the answers as he seemed to. "A library? Of course."

"I'm assuming this building wasn't here when you were a kid, then?" Monroe opened the door and held it for her. "Because you said your mom had to drive you to Duckdale Hollow."

The guy listened, she'd give him that. "Right. The city broke ground for this when I was a freshman in high school."

"Nice."

For being fairly new and having to be constructed on a limited city budget, the building's architecture wasn't bad. Floor-to-ceiling windows allowed plenty of light, and packed wooden shelves full of a variety of genres made Tess happy. At the circulation desk, Tess paused, waiting for Monroe's direction.

"Hi, Tess!" a man of about thirty greeted her, a stack of books in his arms, ready for the self-check.

Her mind scrambled to make the connection. Where did she know him? Client? School? Church? Flipping through memories, she finally snagged the right one. A summer church camp. At a few years older than she was, he'd been one of the counselors. "Oh, hey!" She was about to call him Bryan, but stopped in case she wasn't right.

"How's Ava doing? Is she planning on moving back?"

Oh. One more person who cared more about Ava and if she was going to return than how one of Cobble Creek's own fared. "She's great."

Tess turned her attention back to Monroe. "Which direction?"

Without an audible answer, Monroe pointed toward the children's section with his chin. When they were out of Bryan's earshot, he opened up. "Grab a couple of your favorite picture books—whatever looks interesting."

Perfect. There wasn't anything in the world a little "Cat in the Hat" couldn't fix. "Really?"

She looked over the room with its bold-colored furniture and plush book characters set along the tops of the shelves. The closest bookcase was low to the ground—which made sense considering the typical audience, but it also made perusing the titles a little difficult. "There are a lot of books and authors I don't recognize. Am I really that old?"

"And apparently you don't have as many nieces and nephews as I have. Or else they aren't as rabid of readers."

"I think you mean avid readers," Tess pushed him playfully.

Monroe gave her a half smile. "No, I know what I said. I tell you, these kids practically foam at the mouth as soon as they see me. I'm barely through the door before I'm being bombarded with pleas of 'Read to me, read to me.' On the plus side, that tends to keep me up with current picture-book trends. Very important."

Monroe walked alongside her, sliding an occasional book out so he could see the cover but being selective of the ones he kept. Tess craned her neck to see what he was choosing, but as she did, he slipped them behind his back so she couldn't get to them.

She caught a glimpse of a huge dinosaur in a house on his next selection. "You like those?" She wrinkled her nose. "It looks a little boy book to me." As if any book about boys would be stinky and distasteful. She wasn't one of those girls now, but she easily could have been when she was six.

With a stone-cold, defiant look, Monroe snatched another dinosaur book by the same author and illustrator combination, something about the dinosaur saying something, but he hid it so quickly, she didn't get the whole title. "Just you wait. You're in for a treat." He nodded emphatically. "You'll thank me later."

By the time they had an armful each, Monroe and Tess had to work to keep from being too loud jostling for position at the shelves, each trying to be the first to grab a classic Shel Silverstein. For a Saturday afternoon, the place wasn't as busy as Tess would have expected which was probably for the best considering the number of funny looks they would get from parents.

"I think we've got enough to start," Monroe said, laughing. "Unless you're like my niece Maggie. I can never read enough to her."

"Oh, I don't need many when I've got the best." Tess rushed ahead of him as if it were a competition and she wanted to be the first to sit down. She headed for a low couch on the other side of the children's room, where, she assumed, they were about to read to each other, but as they walked past a huge beanbag beside the bank of windows, Monroe pulled her to a stop.

"What about here?" he asked, boyish grin taking over what she'd once thought was a way-too-serious face.

They settled into the beanbag, feet stretched out in front of them. The natural contour of the bag brought them leaning into each other in the middle, but they had to sit that close to see the pictures together, right?

The whole left side of Tess's body felt warm where her body pressed up against his. Tess's heart sped up at the closeness. Monroe smelled so good—a little like soap with a hint of irresistible cologne and a lot like campfire. It reminded her of Christmas. She breathed in deeply and thought she just might spontaneously combust.

"Why don't you choose one of yours to start?" Monroe said, offering her first crack.

Tess rearranged the slick books at her side, unsure what kind of mood to set. Eventually she settled on one about a boy redesigned the family car. She loved the rhythm of the lines that slipped across her tongue like a brook over smooth rocks. The rhyme of the poetry left her ear and mind satisfied, but the best pat was how the boy took something so familiar, so expected, and made it all that much better.

Tess finished reading, satisfied that it was a good choice, but Monroe seemed far away.

"Monroe?" Tess couldn't believe she'd lost him already. Was the book that much of a dud? Different people had different tastes.

He shook his head, refocusing on her. "Oh, sorry." He flipped through the pages as if trying to refresh his memory. "Good book. It gave me a lot to think about."

Tess chuckled. "Considering a second career as an automotive engineer?"

Monroe closed the book and set it to the side. "Not hardly. But surprisingly, it fits well into my life right now."

She wanted to ask about that cryptic comment, but he quickly moved on with a renewed energy. "My turn."

The book he chose was an irreverent read about a

child painting various body parts. With the sing-song way he read to her, by the time the last part came around, Tess's sides hurt from trying to hold the laughter down to a quiet roar. Tears leaked from her eyes.

"Oh, my goodness, Monroe, you don't set the bar very high, do you?" It was obvious she was being sarcastic. There was no way she could beat that one. She'd have to up her game, use crazy voices or something.

Monroe moved his jaw back and forth like he was holding in his mirth, but his eyes sparked with it. "No pressure, kid." He paused, and the way he looked at her, she had the distinct feeling he thought much more of her than an adult to a kid. "Just choose one."

She blew out a long breath to calm her diaphragm and considered her books. Knowing she could play around with accents, Tess chose one about a Siamese cat who thought he was a Chihuahua who wanted to go into space. You couldn't go wrong with one of those books, even if it was a boy book. About halfway through, Monroe couldn't hold himself back and joined her in reading some of the dialogue with his own goofy accent.

When she finished, he leaned toward her whispering conspiratorially. "Nice job, Tess, but I think you missed your calling as an actress or—" He nodded to a little boy, blue airplane clutched in his fist, who stood watching them. He had to have overheard. "—a preschool teacher." He elbowed her in the ribs, right where she was ticklish, and she squirmed.

With their reading over, the boy wandered off, and Tess whispered back, "Are you flirting with me, Monroe?"

He leaned just a little closer and spoke low near her ear. "I wouldn't do that."

Though clearly, he was.

Did she want him to?

He leaned over the other direction and chose a book with a boring, white cover and words in simple, black type. "It's time. Time for this one." He settled it on his knee closest to her. "But this book is special. Have you read it before?"

She looked at the cover and then back at him. "Why would I? It has no pictures."

He nodded sagely. "I know." He took a serious breath in and then out again. "For this book, I get to read everything on the left-hand page, and you get to read the right. Deal?"

Oh, Tess knew she was being suckered into something, but it was a kids' book. It couldn't possibly be bad, right? "Deal."

By the time they finished reading, Tess could not come up with one single day she'd ever had so much fun. The book was good, the humor unexpected, but it was being able to let go of any adult worries or expectations, and simply enjoy the moments with Monroe as they came. It was a freedom she hadn't felt in a long time.

Tess leaned her head back on the bean bag and closed her eyes. After resting just a moment—enough to get her breathing back to normal after all that laughter—she sat up again.

"I feel like I just finished a workout." She massaged her left side.

"Enough of a workout to replace the missed race?"

She'd almost forgotten about that disappointment. Almost. "Yes. Spending the day with you, reading books," she sighed content with life, "thank you."

"It's not exactly what most engaged people do, you know. We probably should have spent the afternoon shopping for china patterns."

"Are you kidding? This was so much better."

"If you weren't here with me, where would you have spent your day off?" Tess leaned back and crossed her ankles in front of her.

Monroe straightened the stack of read books at his feet. "At the barn. I've got to get that project finished before they call me out. I had to hire help since I don't have the time, what with working so many hours and who knows how soon I'll be reassigned. I don't know what I was thinking when I bought that land."

"Overcome by good looks." Tess tried to pass it off as a joke, not saying whether she meant her own good looks or the beautiful property and barn he'd acquired, but underneath, her blood was starting a slow boil. What had he been thinking buying something he wouldn't even be around to enjoy? It would have been so much better if he'd left well enough alone. If he had, someone else would have bought the barn and property—someone who wouldn't have dismantled her childhood board by board.

Ugh. Why did he even bring it up? She'd been having such a good time. She shifted in the bean bag, uncomfortable in a skirt for such a long time in a low position.

Monroe sunk back into the bean bag. "I have another great idea. Dinner." He didn't sound so convincing. Droopy eyes and a long sigh said something quite different.

She stiffened.

"Are you sure? You don't look that hungry." Conflict swirled inside Tess. Here she'd spent a fabulous couple of hours reading, joking, and laughing with the man of her dreams, only to then be reminded he was also the man who squashed her dreams. Was he really that oblivious to how important that barn had been to her? The least he could do was quit bringing up the subject. As the new owner of the property, it was Monroe's prerogative to do what he wanted with it, but he didn't have to rub it in her face.

She tried to move away so they were no longer touching, but the shape of the bag kept bringing them back together. She studied his charming good looks. With that perfect curly black hair and smoky olive-green eyes paired with the strong jaw and expressive lips, oh, Tess went weak just thinking about him. And then as she had started getting to know the real him behind the stereotype of the firefighter, she wouldn't have been able to resist much longer until he did something to remind him she wasn't supposed to like him.

Monroe's eyes blinked slower each time, and she fully expected them not to open again. She looked at her phone. It was early still.

"How about you rest for a moment while I read the rest of this stack."

"Mmm-hmm." There it was. The eyelids stayed closed. She probably could have spoken gibberish to him and he wouldn't have noticed, so she decided not to tease him—which had to mean she really liked him if she cared that much.

She picked up another book, but reading, remembering when she'd told Monroe about her competition over books with Ava when they were kids, made her sad. Spending the last few weeks with Ava had been unexpectedly fulfilling. Now that they were older and no longer in direct competition for everything, it was easier to appreciate their individual strengths and talents, and Tess realized what a hoot it was hanging around her sister. If nothing else, her time with Monroe had helped her appreciate her time with Ava.

Monroe's phone buzzed in his pocket between them—the perfect excuse for her to jump up, away from him. She stood and whirled around to watch as he answered his phone.

"Scott here," he said, his words slurred in his half-asleep state. He listened, waking more as the split-seconds passed. "On my way."

He hung up the phone. He grabbed the books at his side and then stood. "I guess you heard that."

Tess nodded. "I didn't expect them to call you in after already working a full week." She didn't want to be that kind of fiancée—except she wasn't any kind of fiancée. She had no say in how he spent his time.

"I didn't either, but overtime is always preferable to sleep." He stretched and yawned, which undermined his comment. "I was jonesing for that adrenaline fix only a helicopter and swinging from a rope two hundred-fifty-feet in the air can cure."

Just the thought of it wrenched Tess's middle. If it were her, she would be scared to death, but she was surprised she was worried about him as well.

Being reminded that Monroe was in harm's way every minute he was at work, along with the fact that it took him a long way away from home—both in distance and in time—well, that realization was more effective than being dumped over the head with a bucket of ice water. Monroe wasn't hers. He never would be. He didn't live in Cobble Creek, he didn't even have many hours to spend here, and sooner rather than later he would be sent on to the next fire in California or Arizona or Arkansas, or back to his home. Either way, keeping the relationship focused on the original goal, the fake engagement, was best.

Chapter Twelve

It had been almost two weeks since that library date. Two weeks where Tess tapered down the texts between her and Monroe and deflected questions about wedding details from everyone else. It was important to pull back her feelings for Monroe. There was no point in letting things get out of control.

Instead she occupied as much of her time with summer clients as she could. She'd pictured more girl-time with her sister, but Ava hadn't been around all that much. Ava had been out showing Tyler area attractions hoping for a romantic interlude and proposal. They'd returned, however, with no new relationship news, but wanting to spending time with Tess.

"Of course. I've always loved shopping with you, Ava." Tess peeked into the photo gallery's large window, hoping to see the latest of the creative portraits and stunning landscapes the photographer rotated through.

Today she and Ava were the only ones out on the downtown sidewalks. Not that Cobble Creek had much traffic, except during the fall arts festival or the Christmas season, but typically there was more than this. Summers in Cobble Creek usually held a fairly steady pace of tourists stopping by on their way to either Yellowstone or the Grand Tetons. Nearby wildfires could be devastating to more than just the wilderness.

"What are we looking for?" Tess asked.

There were a few things Cobble Creek excelled at—antiques, local artisans, and anything exuding country charm, like Jessie's amazing quilts—but it wasn't exactly the mecca of shopping for much else, and Ava had specifically said she wasn't in the mood to drive into Duckdale Hollow or Jackson.

"I told you. Wedding stuff." Ava clutched her purse resting on her shoulder, but didn't seem in any kind of hurry.

"Like that isn't vague." Tess shook her head, but loving the easy nature of spending the afternoon with her sister. When was the last time they'd done this? After Ava's first year of college maybe? "Decorations for the reception? A wedding dress? Gifts?"

"Yes." Ava laughed, acknowledging the absurdity of this futile trip. "Ideas mostly, I guess. If I could just get a feel for the style I might want . . ."

"Isn't that what Pinterest is for?" Tess joked. She

threw an arm around her sister in a half hug. "Don't get me wrong. I can't think of a better way to spend an afternoon, and I'm always up for idea shopping, I just don't know this is the place for it."

"I would think you would." Ava pushed Tess away playfully. "Considering you've got your own wedding to plan."

Tess flushed with guilt. She had to tell Ava the truth. It gnawed at her at night when she tried and failed to sleep, lying in bed worrying about all the ways this farce could, and would, go south. But if she admitted she and Monroe weren't actually engaged, there would be no reason for him to come around and see her again. The sale on the property had gone through, and surely, he wouldn't be in the Cobble Creek area much longer. Shouldn't she enjoy it while she could?

"What season are you thinking?" Tess asked, keeping the conversation going. "Would you get married in the spring?"

"I don't think I'm much of a June bride," Ava admitted, "but if that's the only window of time I have, I'll take it." She shrugged and let out a nervous chuckle. "Timing's really going to come down to two things: when, or if, Tyler actually proposes, and when we can fit it in between our residencies and all that. It'll be more of a matter of convenience than anything else." She sighed. "I'm afraid it will seem like we're just fitting it in, but we both really want to do it."

"How very practical of you." Tess would never have assumed that for her sister, but then again, now that she thought about it, it made perfect sense. After all, Ava was the one who read action books, was a champion barrel racer, and had her life scheduled down to the minute practically. She had to with all she was "fitting in" already.

It was Tess who couldn't imagine "fitting in" the wedding for a convenient time. No, when she married, every detail would fit neatly into her grand design. She was the one with the secret Pinterest wedding board.

"And I suppose marrying a wildland firefighter, you'll want a late fall or a winter wedding." Ava stopped in front of Frank & Signs and wrinkled her brow as she looked into the shop's display window. "Wasn't this a welding shop?"

Tess laughed. "When was the last time you were here?" Tess couldn't believe Ava hadn't been here since Frankie had transformed her father's shop. "You remember Frankie Lawson—it's Wells now, but whatever—you remember Frankie from school, don't you?"

"Oh, right." Ava still wasn't making the connection.

"Her father owned the welding shop, but they've expanded the business to include fixing just about anything mechanical you could think of." And even things that weren't, she thought, remembering how Frankie had fixed Tess up with the optometrist Frankie was now married to.

Tess took a deep breath and shrugged off the embarrassment that had shadowed her friendship with Frankie ever since. Tess had voluntarily stepped back from her relationship with Dr. Logan Wells to make way for Frankie, so things weren't exactly strained between them. She just hadn't really spent much time with Frankie since.

Tess tugged on the door and the overhead bell rang a cheery welcome. "Come on. Frankie's is the best place to look for reception decoration ideas. She's a fairy godmother with pretty much anything vintage."

"From welding shop to wedding shop, huh?" Ava looked around with fresh eyes. "Quite the transformation."

Frankie's laugh answered for her. "I've never thought of it that way, but I'd be honored." She stepped forward, coming from her workshop in the back.

Although Tess had expected some kind of adverse reaction to seeing Frankie here in this shop, she found that now, not quite a year later, Tess really was okay with the whole situation. She'd had some fun times with Logan, but she couldn't say she'd actually pined over him. None of their dates had held the spark she'd felt on just that one date with Monroe.

Relieved, Tess allowed her genuine smile to show. "Hey, Frankie, how are you?"

"Doing great, actually." Frankie rested a hand on her

stomach. Was that a slight baby bump? "Harper, come see who's here."

Despite the cool air conditioning, heat flushed Tess's face. Facing Logan's daughter was going to be the hardest hurdle of all. While the girl was sweet and everything any mother would want in a daughter, Tess simply hadn't been ready for that kind of relationship when she and Logan had started dating, so she'd purposely remained aloof from the girl. Not knowing exactly how she felt about Logan, she hadn't wanted to break the girl's heart as well if things didn't work out.

Harper bounced around the corner, goggles fitted across her forehead, pushing up a stray lock of hair, her blue eyes standing out next to her creamy white skin and dark hair. "Tess!" The eleven-year-old ran up and gave Tess a hug that erased the last of Tess's worries.

"We're here for wedding reception ideas," Ava announced, taking over the conversation and causing a tsunami of panic to crash over Tess.

Why hadn't she seen this coming? It didn't take a fortune teller to predict how this conversation would play out, and Tess couldn't think of a single way to prevent it. Not a day went by she didn't think of the fact that honesty would have been the best policy. But she couldn't go back, she could only endure. A couple more weeks…

"Wedding?" Frankie's eyes lit up even as she

scanned both women's left hands but wouldn't see anything.

"Well, it's really more of a research trip than anything," Tess was quick to jump in.

"Don't let her fool you," Ava said lightly, "Tess is engaged, and her fiancé has said he's having the ring custom-made, and I . . . Well, my boyfriend and his best friend went to Constance Diamonds in Jackson today and we all know what that is . . ."

"Best known for custom engagement rings and bridal sets," Frankie finished.

"Sounds like a good sign," Tess agreed.

"Oh, Ava, that's great!" Frankie stepped forward and hugged her, and then stepped back, standing right in front of Tess. "And you're engaged? I hadn't heard! I'm so happy for you!" She folded Tess into a hug as well. As predicted, another huge log of shame was added to the fire in Tess's belly. "Logan's going to be so happy to hear your news! Who's the lucky guy?"

At the mention of Logan, Ava raised her eyebrows at Tess. And there was the second secret up in flames. She probably should have just told Ava that Logan was married—and to their old high school friend, no less—but it simply hadn't come up. On purpose.

Luckily, Frankie was oblivious to Tess's discomfort, and led the women through the store, chatting the whole time. "I have so many ideas... but we need to figure out your style first—colors, textures. Are you thinking a double wedding or two separate ones? Vintage or rustic?"

There were way too many questions to answer, but Frankie seemed to be concentrating on the last of the questions as she pointed to a pair of hearts cut out of reclaimed wood. "I've got this new supplier for my wood—a guy from Idaho named Monroe—"

Ava actually squealed. And Tess had to laugh. *Sure, why not? Bring it on.* She had no pride, no secrets left to hide. She couldn't think of anything more embarrassing than Frankie finding out she was pretending to be engaged. Tess would never be able to show her face around Cobble Creek again when the truth came out.

"Monroe is Tess's fiancé!"

Tess felt sick to her stomach. Would the eventual end of their engagement hurt Monroe's wood business? This arrangement wasn't supposed to be difficult on him. It was amazing what kind of unanticipated casualties came at the expense of this one lie.

Frankie turned an approving eye on Tess as if to reassure her she'd made a good catch. "Then you definitely need to go with the reclaimed wood."

Tess hadn't thought about it before, but if there really were a wedding, reclaimed wood should have to be a given. She looked around until she saw the most beautiful clock. With old barn wood as a background balanced by a more traditional, ornate frame, the clock was beautiful. She ran her fingers along the edge.

"Especially if you make things like this for us." Tess allowed herself a couple seconds' worth of picturing what a wedding to Monroe might be like. "This would be perfect."

"Tess, did you see this?" Ava called from the other end of the room. Apparently, she wasn't as interested in the reclaimed wood as Tess found herself. Tess glanced over to see an antique dress form modeling a beautiful vintage wedding gown. "You've got to try this on. It would look amazing on you!"

With a full tulle over satin skirt and lace bodice, the dress was indeed gorgeous. Tess walked over and fingered the lace cap sleeves. It was delicate, yet strong at the same time. Perhaps it was the idea that it had survived much in its years. It took her breath away.

"When did you start carrying vintage clothing?" Tess scanned the rest of the room, reassuring herself this dress was indeed out of the ordinary.

"Oh, it was the dress form I wanted." Frankie did a half-shrug. "But when the seller offered the dress as well, I knew I needed to make an exception. I had a feeling it would find the right bride." Frankie paused just long enough for Tess to find herself extending her wedding daydream to include this dress. "It would look amazing with your hair. You've got to try it on, just to see, at least." Frankie slipped the dress off the form and draped it over her forearm. "Come on. You can change back here."

THE COMBUSTIBLE ENGAGEMENT

Back in the storeroom, each of the women chose a post—Ava at the back door, and Frankie and Harper at the front. With their backs turned, they gave Tess her privacy as she changed.

"Okay, you can turn around," Tess said, running her fingers over the beads on the bodice. She'd never felt more like a princess. "Ava, could you button the back?" Waiting, Tess felt delicate and beautiful, and she rocked her hips to make the skirt sway.

Ava blew out a sigh. "Hold still, sis, or I'll never get this thing buttoned." Tess tried to remain patient as Ava fumbled at a few more of the buttons. "It will take a year to button all of them and nearly as long to unbutton them. Is Monroe a patient man?"

Heat flared over Tess's cheeks and throat, but she would choose to ignore the comment. "I don't suppose you have a mirror somewhere?" she asked Frankie.

"Do we have a mirror?" Frankie asked Harper sarcastically with a wink. The two of them took off and brought back a standing oval mirror, the wood frame refinished with a coat of white paint and then distressed. She set it in front of Tess.

Frankie checked the time on the wall of clocks over her shoulder. "Sorry, ladies, Harper and I need to run next door for a few minutes. Do you mind?"

"Of course not." Tess waved off the concern. "We'll be here." She smirked at Frankie. "Unless you newlyweds take too long saying goodbye. In that case, I'll text you and let you know what we decide."

Frankie and Harper exited the back door to the alley, and Tess turned her attention to the full-length mirror. The mirror itself was a work of art. Tess leaned forward to touch the gilded frame, but caught sight of the dress and stood back admiring it. Light from a high window turned a few of her auburn strands copper as they draped over the shoulders of the sweetheart neckline, and she gathered up her tresses so she could get the full effect of the gown with her hair up.

Ava fiddled with the last of the buttons, and turned Tess around so she could see the back. The long line of pearl buttons added a simple elegance to the form, and Tess hardly dared to breathe. If she were actually getting married, she could picture no better dress. Ava, though, was the one with a wedding in her near future, not Tess.

Trying not to show how much she liked the dress, Tess turned to Ava. "It's pretty. Now it's your turn." She thumbed down the back of the dress, indicating that Ava should start the unbuttoning process.

"Oh no you don't, sister." Ava turned Tess so she was looking in the mirror once again and then stepped back. "There's no way this dress would look as good on me as it does on you. With my skin tone and hair color, I need a true white, but you—" Ava stopped talking and her eyes fell softly on the folds of the fabric and then up to Tess's face. "With your hair, this ivory is absolutely stunning." She sighed. "You look amazing, Tess."

The familiar insecurities surfaced. As the pretty one, Ava could afford to say that, just to be nice. Still, the compliment had been unexpected and sweet.

"Thanks." Tess was considering what else she should say, if anything, when her phone began ringing across the room.

"Answer it," Ava said. "But I'm *not* trying on that dress, and you *are* buying it."

Distracted, Tess went to retrieve her phone. She knew by the custom ring that it was Monroe. Perhaps it was a little early in their non-relationship to give him his own ring, but it was helpful.

"Hi," she said, breathless as she'd hurried to answer before it went to voice mail. "This is a surprise."

Tess hadn't meant it to sound the way it did. It wasn't that she was trying to give him a hard time about the fact that they hadn't seen or talked to each other in days. She knew he couldn't help that with his job.

Tess could only assume the comment confused Ava as well—as if Tess hadn't expected to hear from him.

"I just needed to hear your voice."

Surprise, and maybe something else, fluttered in Tess's chest. Mirroring her feeling, Ava put her hands over her heart with a silent "aw" on her face. The volume on her phone was obviously loud enough for Ava to overhear.

"I'm all about surprises," he continued. "And spontaneity."

Tess could hear the teasing smile in his voice.

Ava nodded vigorously.

Tess wouldn't have wanted to interrupt her shopping trip with Ava, but her sister seemed to be insisting. "What did you have in mind?" Tess asked Monroe.

"A surprise."

She could picture his teasing grin through the sound of his voice. She'd walked right into that one.

"If you've got time," he finished.

Ava nodded deliberately.

"It just so happens I do." Tess turned her back so Ava could start the arduous unbuttoning process.

"Where are you?" Monroe asked.

"Frank & Signs." If she hadn't already known that he was familiar with the place, she might have offered more information than that.

"I'm just down the street. I'll start walking and meet you there in a few minutes?"

"Sounds good." Tess ended the call and tossed it back onto the couch, wishing she could help with the buttons, but knowing she could do nothing but stand perfectly still and wait. "Are you sure you're okay if I abandon you?" she asked Ava.

"I'm perfectly happy. We got a lot done." Ava worked in silence for a moment.

"But we didn't get any shopping done for your wedding," Tess worried aloud.

"Are you kidding? It's given me plenty of ideas and options to consider. And we found you the perfect dress."

Which made the lying to Ava that much worse. Tess's joy at finding the dress, scheduling a date with Monroe, and sharing this time with Ava soured in her stomach as she thought about the deception.

"Ava," Tess had to tell her, "I need to—"

"So?" Frankie burst into the room minus Harper but full of excitement. At least she didn't have Logan with her. The last thing she wanted was to see her ex while she was standing half-dressed in a wedding gown. "What did you decide about the dress?"

"She'll take it," Ava answered for Tess. "And I'll take the mirror."

Tess went through the motions of changing, distressed at the interruption. So much for explaining it to Ava now. There was no way Tess was going to do it in front of an audience, especially Frankie. They may have mended fences, but she didn't need to look any more foolish than she already had in the past year—or any more than she would in the near future when her fiancé left her to return to Idaho.

"Tess needs to run off to meet Monroe, but I'll be

back in a few minutes. I just need to run and get my car to take these home."

"No problem." Frankie took the dress and started packaging it up as Tess and Ava headed for the front door.

Chapter Thirteen

When Monroe saw Tess and Ava walking toward him on the sidewalk, he knew he shouldn't compare the sisters, but he couldn't help himself. It really wasn't fair for a family to have two such beautiful siblings, twins who looked so different, yet complimented each other so well. But to him, there was no comparison. The red hair was the clincher. Ava's strawberry blonde pixie cut was cute, reminding him of the cheerful flames of a campfire, but it was Tess's darker auburn, long and flowing in waves, that captivated him. Coppery-red like flames in the forest shadows at night. The most enchanting, distracting, and intriguing of combinations—flame, night, open space, and the powerful potential it carried. And exactly how he felt about the gorgeous woman walking toward him with a welcoming smile on her face.

Monroe took the opportunity of a long look to

memorize the curve of her cheek, the playful crinkle around her eyes, the gracefulness of her walk. He knew exactly when she caught sight of him. One side of her lips quirked up in a smile she seemed to want to hold back, but it was that lift on one side of her face, the soft acceptance he saw in her eyes, the feeling that she was truly happy to see him that lured him in. Desire raged in his chest. He had to kiss those lips, yet he might never get the chance.

But they had to sell it, right? How would Ava buy into the fake engagement if they never actually acted like they were in love?

How would Tess react if he kissed her right then? He thought about being cavalier about it, walking up to her and sweeping her into his arms, planting one square on her lips. His heart sped up as she neared. He'd never wanted anything else this badly. It wouldn't be fair to her though.

Ava stopped, but Tess took another step toward him, and Monroe closed the gap, wrapping his hands around her waist and slowly pulling her toward him. There was no way he could stop himself from doing it now that he could smell her shampoo and feel her quick breathing, but he would give her every opportunity to pull away if she wanted to. He tucked his chin and lowered his lips, eyes watching hers in question. She could easily turn this into a hug if she wanted, but she didn't duck to the side. Her eyelids fluttered closed and as soon as he felt her lips under his, he allowed his eyes to close as well.

Her lips were soft but accepting under his, a much more active participant than he would have assumed a drama kiss would be. Heat that had nothing to do with the ninety-degree temperature swept over him, and he cradled the back of her head, afraid she wasn't really there. He wasn't imagining it, was he?

It should be a quick hello kiss—they were, after all, on a busy street in the middle of the day—and Monroe had to force himself to relinquish her lips. "Hi," he whispered, checking her eyes to see if the kiss had been okay with her.

"Hi," she whispered back, as breathless as he felt. She went up on her toes and gave him one more kiss, this one more of the peck propriety required, but also an answer to his unasked question. That cinched it. He was a goner. His heart was hers.

He stepped back, tearing his eyes from Tess to Ava for a quick hello. At least she didn't look bothered by their public display of affection. In fact, she seemed pleased. When Tess threaded her fingers through his, Monroe relaxed. "Do you mind if I steal your sister?" he asked Ava.

"Depends. Where are you kids going?"

Monroe gave a half shake of his head. "No can do. She'll have to fill you in later." He pulled Tess's hand back, causing her to turn toward him so he could appraise her outfit. Her clothes were way too nice for what he had planned. "But first, you need to change." With his free hand, he indicated his own worn outfit. "Clothes you don't care about. The grubbier the better."

Tess raised her eyebrows at him.

"Do you even know my sister?" Ava laughed. "I bet she doesn't own any grubby clothes."

They looked at Tess to admit which of the two knew her better. "I might have something in my closet. From when I painted my front room..."

"Wonderful."

Tess gave him a dubious look.

"You'll love it." Monroe hoped she actually would. If not, he could make it up to her later. "I've got a flannel shirt in my truck you could use."

"Flannel?" She looked horrified. Was that because of the style or the heat? "I'll melt."

At least she wasn't snubbing his fashion choice. "Not where we're going." It was a pretty good hint, in his estimation.

Ava's knowing smile showed she might be the only one to catch on. To her credit, she didn't enlighten Tess.

"Give the man a shot, Tess. If it's what I think it is, you'll have fun." Ava gave her a hug. "I'll take care of things with Frankie and see you later." She started down the sidewalk the opposite direction from where Monroe had parked. "Have fun, you two," she called over her shoulder.

As he and Tess walked back to Monroe's pickup parked a couple of blocks down, Tess never once dropped his hand, even without the audience. He didn't know who she was trying to fool, but it just might be him. If Tess thought he was playing her when he kissed her, she was dead wrong. He wasn't playing. Not anymore. And after that steamy kiss they'd shared, his new mission was to make sure it happened again, for real and without an audience. One way or another, Monroe was going to get Tess to want him to stick around Cobble Creek, and for her to want to stick around to have him.

❁

It hadn't taken Tess long to change into jeans that fit just right and a red V-neck T-shirt that would look great under his red and blue plain flannel . . . if they ever found the darn cave. After driving around the barren countryside in some remote foothills off Highway 280, Monroe backtracked to the one point he knew for sure. If his cartographer had anything right, it would at least be the mile marker, right?

"Here." Monroe pushed the hand-drawn map toward Tess and away from him, not wanting to look at it any more. "See if you can figure this out." He wanted nothing else to do with it. "Just tell me where to go."

Ha. He knew better than to say something like that

out on the line. Firefighters weren't the cleanest group, including their language, and would only have been asking for someone to expound upon.

"You're the expert, I'm sure," he said. "Realtors need to be able to find their way to anywhere; I on the other hand, just get dropped off wherever I'm wanted." Usually in places exactly like this. Except that you could never get lost when there was a big wall of roaring flames in front of you and an even bigger cloud of smoke. But she had to pick out new destinations every day.

The paper crinkled as Tess took the paper. She flipped it around a couple of times, consulted the map on her phone, and enlarged the image until she seemed satisfied. Maybe the maps resembled each other at least a little bit now?

"We got this."

Her announcement brought with it a nice sense of relief. He appreciated her optimism, because they only had a couple of hours of good light left, and he'd really been looking forward to this outing.

"Turn right there." She pointed to her right.

With no heads-up, he slammed on the brakes so he wouldn't pass it completely, and the pickup skidded on the hard-packed dirt. He eyed where she pointed dubiously. "You're saying it's that? It's a cow trail."

She smirked at him. "No, it's not. An ancient ranch road, maybe, but I say we try it."

He backed up so he could turn. "You're the boss."

"I prefer the term Your Highness, the Royal Navigator. Or just Navigator for short."

He bumped along the road, taking it slower than before despite the nagging worry about forfeiting their time. Between the potholes in the road and Tess's knack of telling him to turn at the last second, he couldn't go any faster.

"Thanks for coming out here with me," he said, resisting the urge to squeeze her knee. No matter how playful he'd want it to come across, he was afraid it wouldn't. "I really needed to get away from it all."

She scoffed. "And coming out here is getting away from it all? Isn't this basically where you are all day, every day? Out in the middle of nowhere?"

"Sure, it is." How could he explain it was completely different, and it was all because of her. "Good company. Quiet. Away from the stress and worry. Yeah. This is away."

She directed him around a couple more turns. "Does that mean the fire isn't going well? Is that why you needed to get away?"

"Eh. They thought the fire would be more under control at this point and that the helitack unit would have been sent home by now. They've brought in several hotshot crews from around the country, but this fire is like a hydra. Every time we cut off one head, so to speak, two or three fires pop up." Monroe raked his hand through his hair. "I hate that there's only so much my crew and I can do at this point. Helitack is supposed to stop the small starts before they spread, but we're just not able to get ahead of this. It's bigger than I've ever seen. So now we're relegated to EMS services for injured crew members, and restocking their supplies. You know, more of a support role, and I hate feeling underutilized."

"I'm sorry. That sounds frustrating." Tess paused a beat, but he could tell she had more to say. "Be looking for a left turn up here. Maybe after that outcropping of rocks?"

She lifted a hand to shield the sun from her eyes. It really was getting late in the afternoon. This probably wasn't such a great idea now. Because he had head lamps for the helmets he'd procured, they'd be fine in the cave. And the temperature and lack of light wouldn't change no matter the time of day. It was the having to drive in the pitch black he didn't want to risk. The trip was hard enough with some light.

Monroe thought of all the search and rescue calls he'd been on. He'd rescued plenty of stranded or injured hikers over the years, and because of that, he'd tried to prepare, bringing a well-stocked first aid kit, the right equipment for spelunking, and food. He'd not only packed a sack dinner for the two of them, but he had extra water and snacks just in case they got stranded, as she called it, "in the middle of nowhere." But this close to a main highway, that would be pathetic. Even if the roads resembled a six-year-old's treasure map, criss-crossing and dead-ending randomly in such limited acreage. If all else failed, he'd make his own road, because there was no way he would admit to Reggie that he couldn't follow the map out.

"What's the difference between helitack and hotshot?" Tess picked her way around a particularly large sagebrush, eyes on the ground.

"Hotshots are ground crews on the front lines. They are specially trained because of how dangerous their job is right there in the fire. They dig fire lines and start backburns to direct the fires the way they want them to go and so that they will eventually burn themselves out because the hotshots limit access to more fuel." Dry shale shifted underfoot, and Monroe paused for a second to figure out how best to explain his job.

"At times, helitack does what hotshots do. We're the first to a new fire, we assess the situation from the air, try to fight it if it's small enough, but if we can't control it, hotshot crews and engines are called in. Then we go to more of a support role."

As he spoke, Tess's eyes went wide like she wanted to know more, and he could talk about his job all day long.

"Have you ever wanted to work hotshot?" In her innocence, Tess wouldn't know she was hitting pretty dang close to a nerve. One he tried hard to protect.

"At one point." Memories flooded over Monroe. Those days his crew was training to be hotshots were some of the toughest physically he'd ever known. The work was rewarding and surviving the challenge was quite the rush, but having to use his EMT training to save his best friend turned out to be more than he'd bargained for. "Our crew was so close to becoming certified hotshot when one sudden wind change ruined everything for us."

He gulped, swallowing the pain. It had been years. He ought to be able to talk about it without emotion. Seconds of silence ticked by, conveying what he couldn't in the thick quiet. "I was able to save my buddy, Nick, but he was never the same. That's when I knew I wanted to be part of protecting the land but also protecting the crew members. Helitack gives me the opportunity to meld all of those—I get to work the line with hard, physical labor, I get to get my adrenaline pumping with a good rappel into places people could only dream of seeing, and I get to rescue the injured."

Tess's fingers were clenched together, red marks from each fingertip in contrast to white knuckles of pressure. Monroe stopped the pickup and turned to face her, placing his own hand gently over hers.

"One side-effect of me being in helitack is that my job is less dangerous than it was as a lineman. And remember what I told you?" Monroe was surprised at the fear he saw in the squinted strain around her eyes. "I told you protecting personal property is nowhere near as important as protecting human life—and that includes every one of our crew. We don't do anything to risk lives if we don't have to."

He waited until she nodded. "I *am* careful, Tess." He had to lighten the mood. "My mother would kill me if I wasn't." Tess smiled in response, but it wasn't until he could feel the tension in her hands decrease before he put the pickup back into drive. "Now which way?"

"Up ahead where the road is a little wider? It looks like a few cars have parked there before." Tess set the map on the dashboard before leaning forward to peer out the front windshield. "Except I don't see anything that looks like a cave."

"Reggie said we wouldn't be able to see it until we were standing over the hole in the ground." Monroe was hopeful for the first time. He drove forward and parked. "It's straight down to begin with, and there aren't any markers. But he did say it was close to the parking spot, so let's see if we can find it before we unload all our gear."

As they started walking, Monroe was feeling more and more duped. "I better not have been sent on a snipe hunt or Reggie will have to watch his back next time we're out on the line." He wouldn't actually do anything dangerous, he'd probably just make him pay with extra chores and a chewing out.

After trekking all over the surrounding hills, Monroe

stopped at the top of one, ready to admit defeat. There was no indication that the mouth of a cave was anywhere nearby. He stood, arms folded over his chest, looking into the rapidly descending sun, his hopes for this date plummeting with the warm orb.

Tess walked up to his side, silently surveying the land with him. After a few moments, she motioned across the wide expanse in front of them. "Someday, Homer, all of this could be yours."

The woman knew how to dispel the frustration that had been building in his chest. He put his arm around her waist. "Yes, someday, Martha, we'll build our house right over there yonder, on that there valley next to the creek," which he pronounced as *crick*. "Together, we'll have it all."

Peace settled into his heart. Weeks ago, he'd changed his mind from tearing down the barn to preserving it as his warehouse. He and his buddies worked on it a couple of days, but seriously didn't have the time. And the thing was, the more he got to know Tess, the more he felt how important the barn was to her. That was when he made the crazy decision to work with the Steger brothers in transforming the structure into an actual house. He'd felt good about the decision personally, but worried how Tess would take the news. Until that first book she read to him about the boy who wanted to build a car that could do everything. That had felt like a sign. A sign that she would be okay with his outside-the-box idea.

Every time he thought about telling her about his change in plans or showing her what was going on at the barn, he couldn't allow himself to do it. If she thought he was doing this for her, she could feel pressured into a relationship with him, and even he wasn't sure he was sticking around. His life, his family and his job, were in Spence, Idaho, five hours away. And Tess hadn't wanted a real relationship with him. She'd made that clear from the get-go.

When they designed the layout, Monroe had included as many of the features Tess mentioned she liked when they'd been house hunting as he could, while still incorporating his own tastes. He wasn't building Tess a house, exactly, but her ideas had imprinted themselves on him. When she'd joked that their tastes were opposite, it felt like a challenge, and he was going to show her how together they could plan a pretty great house. The Steger brothers had agreed, and Monroe was thrilled with how great it was turning out.

Okay, maybe he was building this house for her, but he wasn't crazy enough to think it was for the two of them together. He would have it built and then put it up for sale and move back to his job and home base. If Tess liked it, she could buy it.

The thing was, Monroe hadn't been able to stop

thinking about her since their library date. He wished he'd had more time to be with her, but trying to prepare the house, and of course working more hours than anyone should, he'd been strapped. Almost to the point that he'd started to wonder what she thought of him. And yet, here she was, doing something her sister made perfectly clear Tess didn't do, and she was being such a great sport about it. It gave him hope that she could adapt and accept what he was doing to her grandfather's barn.

Holding Tess this close, even if they were both looking off toward the setting sun instead of at each other, brought to mind that amazing kiss only a few hours before. Should he bring it up? Did he owe her an explanation? Would she want to talk about it? Should he pretend it never happened, or that it was all part of the show? Because it certainly wasn't show for him.

Or should he assume it was as consensual as it felt, and try again?

"You wouldn't want to live out here though," Monroe said as a way to distract himself from these lines of thinking. "Didn't I hear you're looking to move away from Cobble Creek? I think I asked you before and you didn't answer, but why? Why do you want to leave?"

Maybe her answer would help him sift through his ever-changing feelings on the subject of relocation and career and home.

Tess was contemplative and he wondered if he'd

lost her, until she finally answered. "I'm trying to decide if it's Cobble Creek or small towns in general." She paused again, and he waited while she weighed her feelings. "Maybe it's neither. I guess it's just that I watched Ava go away to college and stay away, and I felt... left behind in a way. I mean, I've lived in Cobble Creek my whole life, and I have to wonder what I'm missing out on, what I'm giving up by staying here. I know it sounds pathetic, and I don't mean it that way. Obviously, I'm not trapped here or anything and I was —*am*—planning to leave, it just was never the right time. But sometimes when I see that everyone else has moved on, I feel sort of..."

When she didn't finish, Monroe filled in what she hadn't said. "Abandoned?"

Tess shifted, and then sat down on the hard ground, crossing her feet in front of her. "Yes. Kind of. I had with Ava before, but maybe that is changing." She stopped talking, and he allowed her a moment to reminisce. "And with everyone else in town, I feel almost unwanted. It's like they wish Ava was the one here instead of me."

Monroe wasn't sure how to respond to that. "I don't get that impression at all."

Tess stiffened. Yikes, that was the wrong thing to say.

"You talk about what you're giving up if you stay in Cobble Creek," he continued, "but have you considered what you'd be giving up if you left?" Like the closeness she shared with her family, and a thriving business of her own. But it was time to change the subject. "I'm going to run back to the truck for our dinner. I'll be right back."

If he took a straight line back to his truck rather than the circuitous one they'd used to get to the hill they were sitting on, it wasn't that far. Monroe returned with a small cooler and an old blanket to sit on.

"What do we have?" Tess peeked into the cooler, and for the first time, he wondered if he should have planned something different.

"I hope you don't mind tuna." He reached in to pull out two sandwiches cut diagonally in half. He'd been so excited to have soft bread and a "homemade" meal, he hadn't taken into account that it was the kind of sandwich not everyone appreciated. He pulled out small bottles of Sunny D, and realized it probably looked like a sixth-grader packed their meal. He was so used to eating MREs that this passed for a balanced meal to him, or maybe even a treat.

"Sounds great." Tess took the sandwich and drink gratefully.

After a sip of the liquid, she unwrapped the sandwich and took a bite. He attacked his own with gusto, taking at least two bites before he realized that Tess had slowed down.

He raised his eyebrows. "Something wrong?"

She took another bite, chewed, and swallowed before answering with a laugh. "I think you meant to ask if I like Miracle Whip sandwiches with tuna flavoring." She pulled out a pickle from the bag he had in the cooler and took a bite.

"That bad?" Oops. He should have known better. He should have tasked her cousin at Tony's Diner with making the sandwiches. Anthony would have known what Tess would like. Instead, he'd gone with what was available.

Tess took a drink of the Sunny D and smiled. "Are you kidding? I never would have paired syrup-y sweet orange-flavored drink with fish-flavored salad dressing on my own, but as hungry as I am, it tastes great."

In response to her teasing, Monroe threw her a hard glare. "Ah, now you're just being mean."

"I'm serious." Tess took a huge bite, but then covered her mouth with her hand while she finished her thought. "Thank you for this."

And he felt exactly the same way. Even if they didn't find the cave, it had been a win of an afternoon.

Chapter Fourteen

Tess shook her phone awake, looking again to see if Monroe had texted. She'd been so busy the last couple of days with clients and closings, she hadn't been keeping track of Monroe's work schedule. When she looked at a calendar, though, she realized it had been another couple of weeks since they'd seen each other.

In the past, even on the days he'd been working, Monroe had carved out enough time to text her, but even that had slowed way down. The guy made no sense. When they spent time together, he seemed he was one hundred percent present, and she had thought maybe he'd been interested in pursuing a real relationship with her. That kiss had felt far more real than a part in the play to convince Ava, but because she'd chickened out from asking him, she couldn't know for certain.

And then when she heard he'd stopped by the phar-

THE COMBUSTIBLE ENGAGEMENT

macy and chatted with her dad, or when Uncle Gary said he'd seen his truck in front of Hammers Hardware and Monroe hadn't bothered to come see her, what else was she supposed to believe? It had gotten to the point that the family was starting to doubt the engagement.

"Where's your ring?" Aunt Marlene had asked. "How long does it take to get custom made? Are you that picky?"

Have you set a date? her mom texted just about every day.

Even the Wilsons, who had closed on their house and moved in already, had seen Monroe when Tess hadn't. While she was pleased he found a way to live up to his side of the bargain, it hurt that when he stretched his time so thin, he left her out of the picture entirely. Obviously, she wasn't high on his priority list. She couldn't do this much longer.

Tess stared at her phone. Her thumb hovered over his name in her contact list. Monroe was probably exhausted, and Tess needed to respect that, but it wouldn't hurt to send a teensy, tiny text, right? He could respond if he was awake or ignore it if he was busy.

I wish I could say I had more homes for us to look at, but I think you've seen everything, Tess texted.

House shopping with Monroe had been an experience. No one had ever made her laugh about a cockroach infestation like Monroe had. And then some of his design ideas were amazing. When he'd said reclaimed wood, all she could think of was rotting wood, all splintered and cracked, nailed onto a wall, but what he'd described was so much better in person.

Ah, but you haven't seen everything yet, came the reply.

Oh really? Tess knew she was easily baited, but she was already dying to know what he was talking about. You better not be talking about your tent at base camp.

Nope.

Could she get nothing better than this out of him? You aren't cheating on me with Stan, are you? He's the only other realtor in town.

Yeah, no. I have no realtor but you, my darling.

Are you talking a house-house? Or are you just getting my hopes up?

Don't ask questions around Christmas.

Not that again. She'd have to pump him for more information.

How about an unrelated question?

It's still a question.

She decided to ignore that and see if he would answer anyway. I miss my fiancé. In fact, my family is starting to wonder if we're still together. My dad was wondering if I could spell him at the soda fountain tonight so he could take Mom out for a movie date.

Are you inviting me to come along?

Ever worked in a soda shop?

And be a soda jerker? That means I'd be a slob.

Are you quoting "West Side Story" to me? That was incredible. And creepy.

I have sisters, remember, and a mom who is a musical theater buff.

LOL.

If I admit I have no experience, are my chances of getting the job shot?

Was he trying to get out of it? Uh-uh, no way she was going to let him off so easy. Oh, contraire. Everyone should have such an opportunity.

They set a time to meet at Graham's Pharmacy, and Tess was finally able to concentrate on scheduling appointments for a new client.

❁

Over the course of the weeks Tess had known Monroe, she'd seen him in several variations of the mountain man look, and while she liked the rugged side of him, when he walked into Graham's that night freshly shaven and wearing a nice button-down shirt, she literally got weak in the knees. She was glad no one was in the store to witness said event, and hoped she'd camouflaged it well enough that he didn't notice either. Tess couldn't remember ever having that reaction to a guy before, and it kind of bothered her. What, was she some teenager with a crush? It wasn't even real.

"Hey, Sugar," Monroe said, teasingly. He walked

straight to her and folded her into a hug. He had that same heavenly smell she now associated with their library date—that same mix of earthy aftershave, a sharp soap, and the ever-present smoke that was probably part of his DNA at this point. He stepped back from the hug. "I was trying to figure out what endearment I should call you. Engaged couples do that, right?" He waited and she nodded. "I decided I couldn't call you Candy because this isn't a candy shop."

"There's always Sweets. That's generic enough."

"Too . . . expected," Monroe said, retreating even a few more steps as the shop door opened.

Bear and Maddie walked in, chatting about a movie they must have just watched, and Tess realized she hadn't given Monroe the penny-tour yet, let alone the dime-training. "Hey, guys. Good to see you."

"Good to see you too. I hear congratulations are in order." Maddie beamed at them as she clutched Bear's hand. They were the most adorable couple ever. "Are your parents out tonight?"

"Thank you." Tess gave Monroe what she hoped was an endearing, loving look, though something was up with him tonight. Yes, he'd teased her. Yes, he'd hugged her. But something wasn't right. "My parents couldn't interest any of their normal workers in covering the shift tonight, but it doesn't happen too often, so I don't mind."

THE COMBUSTIBLE ENGAGEMENT

Tess grabbed Monroe's hand and dragged him behind the counter as the couple sat across from them. "Watch one, do one, okay?" she whispered, knowing Maddie and Bear wouldn't mind. "How may we help you?" She knew Bear had a thing for egg creams, but Maddie was the wild card. There was no anticipating her order.

"Not sure yet," Maddie said, perusing the board above Tess's head.

"No problem." Tess smiled, satisfied she knew Maddie well. "Take your time."

While she was deciding, Tess showed Monroe where everything was. It wasn't like they had that much to choose from.

Monroe ran his palms along the cool onyx bar top. "I still can't believe this place exists. I don't think I've ever seen an old-fashioned soda fountain."

"Dad couldn't bear to rip it out, so he just built the store around it." Tess placed her own palms on the counter. "This part has been basically the same since 1929. We still have the original soda pulls for seltzer, Coke, Sprite, root beer, Dr. Pepper, and ginger ale. Everything else is mixed from seltzer and syrup. The freezer is small, so we only have the requisite chocolate and vanilla, the must-haves for the 'cow' sodas."

Monroe nodded his understanding, but Tess couldn't show him how to make anything until Maddie ordered.

"What did your nephew have last time we were here, do you remember, Bear?" Maddie asked.

Bear was so good with his nephew, and one day would be a great dad. Maddie had found a good guy. Kind of like Monroe. She'd seen him with her younger cousins and niblings, he was a natural. What was it with her? A year ago, parenthood had been the last thing she wanted. Now, as she saw Monroe joking with Bear and reveled in Monroe's easy manner with everyone, she could imagine being with him in any situation. What would it would be like to have this man by her side for real?

And yet part of her wondered if any of this was for real. He was so good at this fake engagement, even she was beginning to wonder. Sure, he seemed so nice to everyone, but when it came to her feelings, what was most important to her, he was callous and dismissive. He'd bought her family's property and ripped it apart without caring what it was doing to her on the inside. The two of them hadn't had a real conversation about it for a while, but what was the point? She imagined demolition was well beyond complete. But could she continue to tamp down her frustrations and the niggling feeling that, once again, she was the subordinate in a relationship.

And then he kept talking about leaving soon since fire season was almost over. Well, let him go.

"Ever tried the Boston Cooler?" Tess asked her.

When Maddie shook her head, Tess explained. "It's ginger ale and vanilla ice cream."

"That sounds amazing. Refreshing in this heat. Yes, please."

"Egg cream for me," Bear piped up, and Tess talked Monroe through the simpler recipe, the Boston Cooler, as she filled Bear's order.

As the evening wore on, other community members trickled in and out of Graham's, keeping up the steady stream typical of a Saturday night.

"I bet it's great having Ava home," Tess's second-grade teacher Mrs. Jameson said when she and her family had come in for malts and milkshakes. "How long will she be in town?"

Ugh. All about Ava. Again. Over and over and stinking over. Well, Tess was over it. Maybe it really was time to leave Cobble Creek. Then she wouldn't be stuck on a Saturday night mixing up ice cream floats like a teenager with no real job pretending to be engaged while real life swept on past her. If she was going to really patch things up with Ava, the only way she could do that was to leave the town that needled her about her perfect sister every couple of seconds.

"She and her boyfriend had a long break from medical school this time around, but only a couple more weeks, I think. Maybe less," Tess replied as politely as she could. It was only the fourth or fifth time someone had asked her since they'd gotten there.

"See? They never ask about me," Tess hissed as she passed Monroe the stainless-steel mixing cups with the various milkshakes so he could pour them into frosty glasses.

"Perhaps they're asking what they think you want to talk about," Monroe suggested. It was an interesting idea. Rather than assuming that they only saw Tess as part of a pair. "We've had at least as many people ask about or congratulate us on our engagement. Probably more."

They delivered the drinks and turned to clean off the bar where another family had just left.

"Small town gossip. It spreads like wildfire." Tess gave Monroe a significant look.

His perfect eyebrows pulled together and a slight frown crossed those kissable lips, proving she needed to do this and now. Bouncing from thinking about whether or not he would make a good dad to the strong attraction she felt for him proved it.

"We have to do this sometime, and this might be the best place." Tess wasn't exactly happy for the fallout that was sure to come. When she'd made the plan, she had hoped to contain the damage, hoping only family would know, but Monroe hadn't left as soon as she'd expected him to, and at this point everyone in town —*everyone*—would know she had been dumped. Again. "Just one more reason to leave Cobble Creek," she said only loud enough for him to hear.

"What? Because people care? Is that a reason to leave?" Monroe's tone was so light, Tess wondered if he'd gotten the gist of what she didn't want to spell out in front of an audience, but she decided to see how the conversation progressed.

"If I lived in a city, people wouldn't know these things about me."

"That is true. Living in a city can be quite lonely. Almost as lonely as moving from one small town to another, never staying long enough to develop friendships where people care what's going on in your life." Monroe took a sip of water from his cup behind the counter. "It's interesting though. In some ways, living in a city is a lot like living in a small town that butts up next to the next small town. Your daily activities generally revolve around your one small corner of the city—where you live, where you shop, where you eat—they're typically in the same area. Of course, you venture outside those small community limits when you want to do something special—sort of like leaving Cobble Creek to go to Duckdale Hollow to shop or Jackson for entertainment."

Tess bobbled her head from side to side. Monroe had a point. Except for the point that started this conversation—the shame of her sham engagement overwhelming her. Everyone would know. Everyone. But the worst part was that she would be hurt again. She'd tried hiding the hurt when Ava left, and then when Logan chose Frankie over her. Frankie, the one who had set them up to begin with. And now it was going to happen again. As much as she had promised herself she wasn't going to fall for Monroe, it was too late. His leaving was going to be the hardest of all, and that's what bugged her the most. She wasn't supposed to care.

Monroe stepped around Tess for a pull on the seltzer water for another drink he was mixing, his banged-up knuckles sure of their task. She watched as he continued talking, hardly seeming to pay attention to building the drink, yet anticipating how high the head would grow over the ice cream. He let go at the perfect time, and swished the drink a couple of stirs so the chocolate syrup would mix with the soda water. He'd caught on quickly.

"What did you do to your hands?" Tess hadn't noticed the bruises and scrapes before. "Occupational hazard?" *Or demolishing my grandfather's barn?* The thought was a heartburn that grew rapidly in her chest.

"If you're talking the firefighting, no, not really. It's from working out at the property." He gave his hands a cursory glance, and a stupid grin so wide he could have been on a billboard for an orthodontist filled his face. Tess's heart thumped with rage. He passed the drink off to the customer. "Is there anything else we can get you right now?"

When his date shook her head, the teenager said no,

and he grabbed two straws.

Monroe turned back to Tess. "The splinters are the worst. Having to dig in to get them out." His not realizing anything was going on with her made her even angrier. He cleaned off the prep area with a towel. "I'm surprised how business has taken off in the area. I can't believe how many contracts I've gotten in the past two weeks alone. I guess word spreads fast when ranchers hear there's someone willing to pay good money for old wood. New fences and sheds will be popping up all over the valley." He leaned against the counter, his muscled arms crossed over his broad chest, he was overconfident and a jerk for bringing up the barn and how everything was going his way. An hour ago, she was fixated on Monroe's positives—his good looks and toned muscles, sense of humor and friendly, caring ways—but whatever happened to scruples, common decency, and honoring local history?

"My crew and I will be out at your grandpa's place a lot over the next bit, if you want to stop by." He sounded hopeful.

But that was the entire problem—it was no longer her grandpa's place, it was Monroe's, and she didn't want to see with her own eyes what he'd done as soon as it was his. He'd already told her in uncertain terms.

"In fact, I'm going to need a good realtor to partner with pretty soon." Monroe stepped closer and placed his hand at the small of her back. The gentle pressure at his fingertips guided her to lean into him, and the audacity of the move cracked her calm facade.

Tess stepped back, images of him tearing her grandfather's place apart, ripping at her former happiness. Didn't the man get tired of destruction? How could he spend every day watching forests burn and wildlife die, and then turn around and strip away people's memories board by board?

※

Tess stepping back from Monroe hurt. Had he misread the signs?

Monroe thought back over their light-hearted conversations over the evening—some of them more in-depth than others, but always respectful, always bringing them closer, or so he thought. It was not his imagination that there had been times that Tess had brushed up against him or stood a little closer than necessary, times she'd held his eyes longer than you would with a coworker or friend, times her comments had hinted at more. And then all of the sudden, she seemed put off?

What had he done or said wrong? He scrambled back, trying to remember his last words.

"What are we doing here?" She probably didn't mean why they were filling in for her parents.

If there had been any question if Tess was actually

upset, her practically spitting the words made it painfully obvious how angry she was. She meant their relationship.

Monroe took a calming breath, hesitating to keep from, exploding. "If you remember correctly, this was your idea."

Well, not technically. He was pretty sure she'd made it clear the engagement would be fake, and over the past couple of weeks his feelings had gone way past fake and somehow had become the real deal.

"No," Tess countered, "my idea was to pretend, not to involve the whole community in this sham."

Oh, so it was her pride in the balance, not her heart. Why could he never find a woman as invested in the relationship as he was?

"What did you think was going to happen, Tess?" He kept his back to the customers, whispering and working to keep a smile on his face. "Of course, the town would find out about the engagement. Everyone knows you. Everyone here cares about you and your family, and they want you to be happy. These people were happy for you."

And he'd been naive enough to believe they were on their way to being happy together for real.

His jaw clenched at the frustration of it all. "You know, if you hadn't been so jealous of Ava . . . if you hadn't been so childish and vindictive in the first place, this never would have happened."

Tess's face flushed. He'd gone too far.

"And there you go, taking Ava's side. Of course you would—just like everyone else—and you don't even know her."

Who was she to talk? Tess didn't know the people in this town and she didn't know her sister, so what had made him think she would know him at all? Still, the betrayal burned. He'd been nothing but loyal to her.

"That chip on your shoulder is pretty deep—a hole you may never get out of." He took some of the used ice cream scoops and walked to the back corner, away from the customers to clean them. Tess followed, as he knew she would. "I know you won't believe me when I tell you this, but you are the only one comparing you to Ava, and you need to stop. It's like you're so busy digging a firebreak to keep from getting burned, that you've isolated yourself so well that you can't even be touched." He glanced at her sideways, trying to gauge her reaction, but her poker face was pretty good. "It sounds like a pretty lonely place to be."

He knew all about being lonely, and wondered if it was as much the product of his own choices as hers were for her. Gloom settled over him. He didn't want to fight, but he couldn't do this either—this being afraid to tell Tess what was on his mind, this having to listen to her talk about how she would never be as good as her sister. Life was not a competition. It just wasn't.

"You know what?" Tess's chin came up defiantly,

her eyes steely on his. "Maybe we just need to end this engagement now."

It was futile. If there was one thing Monroe had learned in his time in the forest service, it was that sometimes you had to start fires to end them. Sacrificing small portions to save acres more. Perhaps he and Tess could have been good together, but more likely, it would have crashed and burned sooner or later. How could it not, the way they started out? It had always been the plan. Why not end it now and prevent the compounding costs later?

Monroe untied his apron and folded it. "If that's the way you want it, maybe we do."

He was pleased that he never raised his voice, but the intent of the conversation—who was he kidding, that was a full-blown fight—would have been obvious to on-lookers. Which was exactly what was needed. They were ending their façade of an engagement, and Tess needed all of Cobble Creek to know it. He just hoped he didn't look like the jerk he felt. He hoped she came out looking better.

His heart pounded as he stepped from the air-conditioned, clean air of the pharmacy into the smoky haze of the summer evening. He walked down Main Street, passing a photo shop, a hair salon, a bookstore. Leaving was the wrong thing to do. There was no reason to walk out of a simple misunderstanding. At least he had to assume it was simple. And a misunderstanding? For sure. He still didn't get it. But was this something the two of them could talk through if they hadn't had an audience?

No. It wasn't worth it, not since their relationship was only ever meant to be temporary. So he'd been dumb to let a few flirty looks and fun banter give him the idea there might someday be more.

And the further he walked, the better he felt about it. Since he was going to have to leave anyway, he was glad it could be on Tess's terms. She couldn't know it would tear at him like this. But at least this way the community saw that she was the one kicking him out. He wouldn't be another on her list that left her behind.

Monroe would miss her though. Fiercely. He could go back to the property and throw himself into the barn remodel, but the spark of excitement of working on the project would be gone. Still, he'd invested this much, he needed to see it through. He'd have the Steger brothers step up construction and help while he could, but he would never keep it. He'd finish it, sell it, and look forward to moving back to his tiny apartment near family.

There was no reason to live in Cobble Creek if he and Tess weren't going to be together. There was no way in a town this size, he could avoid Tess for the rest of forever. As invested as his heart had been in her, Monroe would be powerless to take on that cavalier, maverick persona he'd worn like armor in the past.

When he got to the end of the shops on Main Street, Monroe turned around and walked down the other side of the street, passing a flower shop, the antique store, restaurants, and the hardware store he spent so much of this money in these days. By the time he reached his parked truck, he'd decided to pound his feelings for Tess right out of his heart. He'd head back to the property for the last few hours of that night and the next running the nail gun or the table saw—anything with power to drown out his frustrations.

A weak part of him wanted to convince Tess to come see the barn transformation, take a moment to examine the blueprints. She would forgive him when she saw what he was doing for her. No. His brain dismissed that as quickly as the desperate thought occurred to him. He wouldn't have the reason they were together to have anything to do with the barn or his pathetic overtures of love. He would simply finish the project and sell it. She'd see it with everyone else when it came on the market.

As much as he loved avoiding town and Tess by staying secluded on his own oasis in the mountains, Monroe was relieved when his supervisor called, starting his next work week with a bang. A change in the fire demanded all-hands-on-deck, and that meant Monroe was safe to leave the barn, Cobble Creek, and Tess behind.

Chapter Fifteen

It took longer than realizing she was alone manning the soda fountain on a Saturday night for Tess to regret goading Monroe to literally throw in the towel, but not much. That weekend was the worst in the history of hot, sticky, too-long summer days in western Wyoming's history. Or at least it was for Tess. Made even longer as she was mired in the molasses of regret and should-haves.

"Time for a pedicure," Ava said, several days later, proving that something must be drastically wrong for Tess's sister to want to cheer her up with what Ava usually said was a waste of time and money. "A little pampering wouldn't hurt."

"Since when would you think that?" Tess asked, noting that she could do with a fresh color on her tootsies, and noticing that Ava's toes were still red, white, and blue from Independence Day almost six weeks ago.

"Since I know my sister. And I think Aunt Marlene would agree."

That brought a smile to her lips. "What salon owner wouldn't agree with that?"

Ava hooked her arm around Tess's and dragged her from moping around her mostly-dead office in the middle of the afternoon. Ava looked at Penny, Tess's part-time assistant. "Do you think we have an hour or two?"

"Easily." Penny flushed when Tess glared at her, not happy to be reminded that summer was ending and the sales season winding down with it. "I'll schedule around, if anyone calls for an appointment. You need this break."

Was she really that pathetic?

"Let's go." Ava put her hands on her hips. "Grab your stuff. We're out of here."

Just opening the door into the thick smoke pouring through the town gave Tess a clue why home visits had dropped so suddenly. Who would want to go walking around random backyards under apocalyptic skies or try examining homes' exteriors if they couldn't see what they were doing, let alone breathe easy.

"At least CC's isn't far." Only a few blocks straight down Main Street. Hearing the whine in her own voice, Tess tried to dial back the complaints. She wasn't the best of company these days.

She'd spent more than enough time analyzing

Monroe's words and stewing over her own until she couldn't even remember the fears and opinions she'd held before their argument. She just couldn't bear think about it anymore.

Stepping into CC's Salon was an odorous relief, even with the sharp scent of chemicals, dyes, and polishes. At least they were out of the smoke.

"Good afternoon, ladies." Connie's strawberry-tipped platinum blonde pixie cut was just the right amount of happy to perk up Tess's mood. "Your aunt ran down to Tony's Diner for a late lunch, but I'm here." She cracked her gum and popped a hand on her hip. "What can do for you today?"

Only one other client was in the shop, sitting under a dryer with her hair in foil wraps, so even without an appointment, this might work.

"Oh, we can see Marlene later. Do you have time for a couple of pedicures?" Ava took charge, as usual.

"Can't think of a better way to pass the afternoon." Connie jumped up from her seat behind the counter.

Tess worked hard to stifle a laugh. A mini jacuzzi soaking her feet in scented water and having her feet massaged with paraffin was pure bliss. This late in the summer, her heels were cracked from exposure and the sweltering heat. But an enjoyable way for Connie to spend an afternoon? For Tess just about anything would be preferable to coddling someone else's stinky feet.

Connie directed them to seats so she could prepare

the water, but Tess excused herself to freshen up in the restroom for a moment before sitting down. As she closed the bathroom door to make her way back, Tess overheard Ava and Connie caught up in the expected conversation about med school and Ava's imminent return to California.

"I bet it was nice to spend this time with Tess. You must hate being apart," Tess heard Connie say as she was about to round the corner. Tess hung back for a moment. For the first time in her life, she realized Ava got it too.

Why was the realization such a shock? Monroe had been right. On every point.

Everything he had told her over the past few weeks. Calling her out for being childish and vindictive had cut her to the core, but perhaps that was truly how she came across. It took seeing herself through an outsider's eyes—once she focused on the truth of the matter rather than the hurt—to see she had been wrong. Monroe had called her out on her weaknesses, but he hadn't done it with a pointed sword. He hadn't tried to hurt her.

"It's been so nice." Ava's words brought Tess back to the present and her sigh made Tess feel all fuzzy and warm. No matter what had happened between them, they were sisters, and close ones at that. "I've missed her. And I loved seeing her so happy with Monroe. I only wish I hadn't had to come during her busy time. She's had an awful lot of clients, but what can you do?"

Tess could picture Ava's signature shoulder shrug and half smile.

"She's really made a name for herself in town. It's impressive," Connie said.

"Yes, she's good at what she does, but then again, she's always been that way—determined, driven, and talented. I knew she'd be successful as soon as she decided to do it."

There was not even a hint of complaint or jealousy in Ava's voice, only pride. Was this how Ava truly felt?

With the lag in Ava and Connie's conversation, Tess knew she'd better make her way to the front.

"There she is," Connie said. She had the tubs filled with sudsy water and waiting for Tess.

Tess took the chair next to Ava, pushing herself back on the slick vinyl and sinking into the cushions. "Oh, I might fall asleep right here." She allowed Connie to remove her sandals and put her feet into the tub to soak, but the whole time, her mind was on the overheard conversation.

"You ladies relax and let the water do its magic while I help Wanda over there. I'll be back in a while."

"Thank you." Tess watched Connie leave. When she was out of earshot, she turned her body slightly toward Ava's. "And thank you." She started to choke up, not knowing how to convey her feelings.

"For what?" Ava opened her eyes and took in her sister's face. Tess felt exposed as Ava's eyes traveled over her every laugh line, every expression.

"For the compliment." Tess kind of felt silly having this conversation, but she felt strongly it needed to happen. "When you told Connie I was determined, driven, and talented." She swallowed. "I had no idea you felt that way."

"What?" Ava seemed surprised. "Of course, I do. You're also the pretty one and the smart one." She smiled as if she were teasing, but it was obvious she meant every word. Growing up, I always had to try harder at whatever I wanted to do so I could be like you."

Tess's first reaction was to dismiss Ava's words as obligation. That was just the kind of thing a sister would say to lift a depressed sibling. But Tess allowed herself a moment for the compliments sink in. Trying to view their shared past through Ava's eyes, Tess saw that she too had talents that Ava might have appreciated as much as Tess had Ava's riding skills and memorization smarts.

"That's exactly how I felt about you, Ava." Tess blinked away a couple of tears. "I never felt I measured up to you."

"Pssh," Ava dismissed it. "One thing I realized recently—we never should have let it be a competition between us."

The realization felt like a fire extinguisher dousing the flames of Tess's jealousy. In a way, it was a relief, but it also left her with a feeling of loss. All those years of slowly destroying their relationship that should have been avoided.

"But not anymore." Tess reached out and grabbed Ava's hand on her armrest.

"Not anymore," Ava echoed and squeezed back. "I just want to see you happy." She sniffled, and Tess fought her own tears again. "And to do that," Ava clarified, "I think you and I need to spend more time together." She sighed. "Except I go home in two days."

Tess would do her best to make sure the next two days were the best she and Ava had ever had. And after that, she would do her best to make sure her relationship with Ava continued to heal. This revelation, brought on by her argument with Monroe was a good start. If only she'd listened to him sooner.

Images flipped through her memory of the times she and Monroe had spent together. When they'd gone house hunting, she knew he was listening closely. He seemed to care about her opinion, and her childhood, and her relationship with books. And then he'd taken what he'd learned to tailor the perfect date at the library. But even when things had not gone exactly as he'd planned and they got lost in the desert, he joked with her, had fun with her, made it a success rather than focusing on the failure of finding the cave.

Monroe had a willingness to try anything—pretend engagements, meeting the family when he hadn't even know her, learning how to concoct brown cow drinks.

Tess sighed. She missed him, pure and simple. She'd been wrong.

She had been happy. And she would be again. Even though she'd tried calling Monroe once already since their argument, pride constraining her from groveling more than that, Tess pulled out her phone to try again. She didn't want to sound desperate, so she opted for a quick text that was anything but quick to compose. After several attempts to write the perfect text, she settled on FEEL AWFUL ABOUT THAT SATURDAY NIGHT. CAN WE CHAT? She hoped it balanced contrition and confidence.

With the weight of her estrangement with Ava now off her chest, Tess felt relief wash over her. "Don't mind me if I fall asleep," Tess warned.

"I won't," Ava said, "because I'll probably beat you to it."

Tess closed her eyes, allowing her thoughts to once again wash over her time with Monroe. Those smoky green eyes with their dark lashes that always held her with so much respect and admiration. His thick dark curls and strong jaw and those oh so kissable lips. Her heart fluttered at the memory of that day on the sidewalk just outside. Her cheeks warmed at the memory of that magnificent kiss. She couldn't give up on him. She just had to figure out the best way to make it up to him.

The heaviness of sleep tugged at her arms, weighing them down on the arm rests, when she heard someone enter the salon. It could be Marlene coming back from lunch or just another customer, either way, Tess wasn't going to spoil her rest by opening her eyes unless spoken to.

"The sheriff—who am I kidding? I can't call him that . . ." A light chuckle followed.

That could only be one person, but Tess opened her eyes to make sure. Jessie Lockheart, the sheriff's wife and owner of the Country Quilt Inn, stood with her back to the glass door, her hands behind her on the push-bar. "Trent wanted me to spread the word. Riverside is being evacuated." She blinked quickly and took a deep breath. "With unpredictable, high winds, the fire took an unexpected turn and is threatening the outskirts of that town. They're in the process of evacuation, but that means some of the residents will be coming into Cobble Creek looking for shelter—"

Jessie held up a finger, pausing her speech, and she pulled out her phone. "I forgot to tell Sheila something else. So many details..." She clicked away on her phone and then looked up. "Sorry. Just trying to figure out where people can stay. We're already booked through the end of summer." She blew out a breath and set a hand on her cute baby bump. "I've got to get back there.

Could you help spread the word? Trent is calling for a town meeting—one of the firefighters will be at the community center at four to brief him and anyone who wants to help is welcome. So far all we know is they're evacuating as we speak, and there's already been one casualty."

Tess's eyes went wide. "Casualty?" She swallowed. "A civilian?" That would be awful.

Jessie shook her head slowly, almost reluctantly. "One of the firefighters." She wouldn't lift her eyes to meet Tess's. "I don't know any names. I'm sorry, Tess." When she finally did look up, her eyes glazed with moisture. "I never should have said anything about that. Try not to worry, and I'll try to find out more details from Trent, okay?"

Tess nodded, woodenly. Maybe that was why Monroe hadn't texted back. Panic struck her in the chest like a hammer. She had to call him. Had to hear his voice. She stood up, barely noticing her feet were still in the pedicure basin. She was lucky she didn't run out the door with wet feet.

"Here, let me help you." Connie grabbed a towel.

"Oh, shoot, umm . . ." Jessie looked at her watch, strapped on to her wrist with several leather cords. "I'm so sorry, Tess . . . and we don't know for sure if the rumor is true."

"Don't worry, Jessie," Ava said. "Tess would have heard one way or another. At least this gives her time to process instead of being blindsided at the meeting in front of everyone. I'm sure Monroe's all right, but let us know if you hear anything."

Tess knew Ava was right and tried in vain to smile at Jessie. It wasn't her fault.

"Go ahead and go," Ava continued to Jessie. "We'll see you at the town meeting?" She waited for Jessie to nod. "I know you've got lots to take care of. See you there."

"Sit down, honey," Ava said once the door closed behind Jessie. She patted Tess's vacated seat. "Connie will get us out of here, and we'll get a hold of Monroe."

Feet dried and pedicures forgotten, Connie practically pushed Tess and Ava out the door. "I can't go to the meeting—" She looked significantly to the woman under the dryer. "—but text me if there's anything I can do, okay?"

Ava assured her they would and put an arm around Tess to guide her through the door. "I know it's difficult, but you need to have hope, Tess. Monroe is good at his job. He knows what he's doing."

The words slid across Tess like a stifling summer wind. She couldn't breathe.

Unaware, or at least not caring that Tess wasn't catching most of it, Ava kept up the constant stream of reassurances. "I know it's awful to think that any of the firefighters died, but it would have to be someone on the front lines, right? What are those groups called? The hotshots? I mean, no one said anything about a helicopter going down."

This line of conversation was even more upsetting than Ava probably anticipated.

"I can't." Tess's throat was closing up, her chest heavy. Was she coming down with a cold? "I can't..."

What she was going to say was that she couldn't allow herself to think of anyone dying in that fire out there—Monroe or anyone else—but the words got stuck in the lump in her throat.

"I texted him just half an hour ago maybe. He hasn't responded." Her voice felt small.

"That makes sense if you think about it, doesn't it? He's got to be working, right?" How could Ava sound so optimistic, as if Tess's whole world wasn't going up in flames. "I'm sure he'll get back to you as soon as his shift is over."

Like he'd clocked in for an eight-to-five job in some safe office cubicle somewhere. Tess let out a wry laugh. "I haven't heard from him in weeks." Ava knew all about how that Saturday evening, and the engagement, had ended. "He never picked up when I called before, and now..." A sob threatened to escape and Tess swallowed it back. "What if I never get to apologize? What if he never knows that I love him?"

Her words came as a surprise to herself, even if Ava didn't react. Tess loved Monroe. She *loved* him.

"He knows that, honey." Ava gave her sister a half

hug as they continued walking blindly down Main Street. "I'm sure you've told him countless times. You wouldn't have been ready to marry the man if you hadn't. He knows your feelings wouldn't change over some silly argument in a soda fountain."

A small tear leaked out of her left eye, and Tess wiped it away quickly. Smoke sure stung. "Ava, there's something I need to tell you." There was no going back now. "Monroe and I . . . aren't engaged. We never were."

Tess's throat went dry. "I just didn't want to be stuck with Glenn for one thing—you do realize he's a complete creep, right? Don't set him up with anyone else. But more than that, I just . . ." She couldn't believe she had to own up to being so petty. "I wanted to beat you at something, and when you said you were about to get engaged, well, it just came out." The confession pumped out of her like a plummeting housing market in a bad economy. "As soon as I said it, I knew I'd made a mistake, but I didn't want to look even dumber in front of you."

Ava stopped Tess in the middle of the sidewalk and hugged her for several long seconds. "Never. You never look dumb to me." Ava released Tess and as she started into Tess's face, Tess felt the tears start to leak from the corners of her eyes.

"I'm so sorry I didn't tell you the truth." She searched her sister's eyes but saw nothing other than compassion there.

"Me too. But . . ." Ava's forehead wrinkled. "Your relationship looked so real. That kiss . . ."

"I know." Tess's cheeks flushed at the thought and she pressed her fingertips to her lips. "That kiss . . ." She could elaborate, but she didn't need to. "Yes, that felt real." She sighed long and hard. "The thing is that somewhere in all that pretending, I thought Monroe and I were starting to make a real connection. Until we 'broke up' last Saturday, and now I can't even get him to respond to my apologies. Ava, what am I going to do? I feel so conflicted. On the one hand, Monroe and I never really had anything, so I have no right to hope he would even try to mend things with me. But on the other hand —" She loved him.

"Nope." Ava stared her down in the middle of the sidewalk, her tone firm.

"Nope what?" The way Ava had said it chased Tess's tears away, bringing out her desire to fight.

"You are not conflicted. In fact, you know exactly how you feel about Monroe Scott, and it's far more real than that fake engagement." Ava's teal blue eyes bored into Tess's. "You can try to fool yourself, but you absolutely cannot fool your twin."

The sisters stared at each other for a few more seconds, relief seeping into Tess's chest. She wasn't alone in this. Nor was she making anything up. Even Ava said her feelings were real.

"And I'm not sorry to say that I think the man feels exactly the same way about you."

Tess cocked her head to the side and started at Ava. "I don't know—"

"I do." Ava shook her head emphatically, and then took Tess's arm again, encouraging her to keep walking. "I've seen how that man looks at you. How he listens to everything you say. How he's willing to try anything for you—didn't you say the two of you cooked curry even though he told you he hates Indian food?"

She was right. Maybe Monroe did reciprocate her feelings—or at least he had at some point. Maybe she could convince him they should try again.

Panic wrung her thoughts with worry again. "What am I going to do while I wait to hear from him? What if he never calls? What if he never . . . can?" The words crashed out of her, but voicing them didn't make her feel any better for it.

Ava squeezed Tess's arm, but her voice was calm, encouraging. "Call one more time, tell him what you've overheard and that you need to find out if he's okay."

Tess nodded once. Yes, she could do that. But what if she had to wait hours for a response? What if it took days? "And until I hear back?" Tess looked into the sky, pleading. "What do I do?"

Ava remained quiet as they walked. Hopefully Ava didn't think it was impossible. Tess was counting on her to help her through this. "Service is the best distraction."

Not even realizing where they were going, Tess allowed Ava to guide her into her office.

"Service?" Tess didn't even have to finish asking the question to have her mind filled with ideas.

Their displaced neighbors. Knowing how much Tess was paralyzed by fear, others had to be experiencing similar worry over the effects of what the fire would do, what it might steal away from them. Tess couldn't fight the fire itself, but she could keep it from winning.

Tess went to the mini fridge in her room and pulled out two bottles of water. She handed one to Ava. "Service." This time she said it emphatically. A mission statement, a motto. "I have some ideas about how we can do just that."

❈

FOUR O'CLOCK CAME FAR FASTER than Tess appreciated, but it also meant that she hadn't spent the last hour and a half fretting. There was no sense making herself crazy over the snippet of so-called information out there. The lack of a return call or text from Monroe during a major work crisis shouldn't be a worry. She and Ava hurried down the sidewalk, ash from the fires swirling down on them like snow flurries with the change in wind. The small-town crowds funneled into the community center where everyone claimed a folding chair to hear the latest news. Worried and excited townspeople spreading the current rumors as they waited.

"Thank you all for coming." Sheriff Trent Lockheart stood behind a couple of folding tables at the head of the multi-purpose room, flanked by Mayor Griff Armstrong and Deputy Benny Gaines. "If this were an official town meeting, we would probably run things differently. This was just the quickest way I could think of to disseminate information. From here on out, you can find updates on the fires at #WolfRidgeFire on Twitter."

Sheriff Lockheart cleared his throat. "None of you will be surprised that part of the reason we're here is because my beautiful bride Jessie thought it would be helpful to organize volunteer efforts for the displaced." He gave Jessie a long look but otherwise kept his professional demeanor. "More on that in a moment."

Most of the town sat in folding chairs, their attention rapt on him as he continued, "I'm sure you've all heard the basics or you wouldn't be here, but we have Assistant Supervisor Johnny Stein, part of the Region 4 helitack crew, here to explain the situation further. Johnny..."

Relief flooded over Tess as she heard the name and saw with her own eyes, Monroe's right-hand man. If Johnny was okay, that meant nothing had happened to their helicopter and crew, though she could use a little more reassurance. It took everything in her to keep from jumping up to ask him if Monroe was all right. Ten more minutes and she'd interrogate Johnny with every question running through her mind.

"Thank you for the intro, Sheriff, and good afternoon, good people of Cobble Creek."

Next to Sheriff Lockheart's pristine uniform, Johnny looked like he hadn't seen a shower in a week. Tess could smell the smoke and sweat emanate from him even from where she sat, and soot covered the back of his neck and in the cracks of his knuckles. He shifted from one foot to the other, changing his hand position in the most distracting of ways. Tess tried to catch his eye, but he wouldn't make eye contact with her. He looked everywhere but.

"As you have heard," he continued, "the Wolf Ridge Fire took an unpredictable turn two days ago, due to high winds. Despite calling in every available crew nationally, the fire has surged from 143,000 acres to approximately 240,000 and is now threatening the small town of Riverside, about half an hour from here."

Johnny wiped a hand over bloodshot eyes. Was that out of exhaustion and smoke exposure or out of sadness?

"Local law enforcement has issued a mandatory evacuation of every Riverside resident for their own safety. While of course many of them will be going to family and friends outside the area, many of the residents do not have a definite destination. They want to remain close to jobs and family even if they are unable to get into their homes. As the next closest town to Riverside, this will place the most pressure on your town's resources, specifically housing. We do not know how long the evacuation will be in effect; there is no way to anticipate this. As always, we will get families back into their homes as quickly as possible, but it goes without saying that safety"—Johnny started to falter—"is of the utmost importance."

Johnny's display of emotion had Tess in nervous knots. There must be some truth to the casualty rumor, and she prayed it wasn't Monroe. Is that why Johnny was here instead of Monroe? Monroe was Johnny's supervisor, so wouldn't it have been Monroe's responsibility to liaise with the town rather than Johnny?

Sheriff Lockheart stepped to Johnny's side, ready to take over the meeting again.

"Jessie?" Sheriff Lockheart invited her up with a wave of her hand.

Jessie jumped up in her usual exuberance. "With getting the word out about this meeting and making sure we're getting things straight with the Inn, I haven't had much time to make a plan. I just knew that many of you would want to offer to help, so I figured if we had a chance to discuss it . . ." She paused, but only briefly. "The most pressing needs will be food and housing. The Country Quilt Inn is booked solid right now, but Sheila and I are checking with vacationers to see if they would rather reschedule. Who is really going to want to stay here with this smoke? No offense—" She raised an apologetic hand to Johnny. "We could possibly cook extra at breakfast and our snack time, but I don't think we'll be able to accommodate many more than we typically do since our kitchen really isn't that large."

Jessie drifted off, as if trying to figure out a plan, and Tess couldn't wait any longer to share hers. She raised her hand, and Jessie nodded in her direction.

"As soon as I heard, I called Stan. As the only two Realtors in town, he and I have been on the phone for the past hour and a half solid getting in touch with clients whose homes are currently vacant. While we wouldn't typically ask this of any client, as soon as they heard, most were willing to allow displaced families to bunk down for the night in their homes."

This procedure was highly irregular, not to mention risky, but the residents—and former residents—of Cobble Creek were generous. "There probably won't be enough houses to cover every family in need, but every little bit would help. Also, there are no appliances or even beds, but it would be shelter and facilities." She looked around the room to see if anyone else had something to offer.

Sheriff Lockheart nodded, and Tess could see the gears of his thought moving as he assessed the situation. "Considering we really don't have many other options, I think it's a generous and thoughtful gesture. Our department will assist by keeping an eye on the properties so that owners don't get taken advantage of. Thank you, Tess. I love the outside-the-box thinking." He turned to Johnny. "Any idea how many evacuees we should expect?"

"No, sir," Johnny said. "I sure don't." He cleared his throat. "But I'm sure Monroe Scott would have offered his property if he were here."

The bottom dropped out of Tess's stomach, but she forced herself to concentrate on what Johnny was saying. It took everything she had in her to keep from asking about Monroe. Was he okay?

"Several families could bunk out at Monroe's place on County Road 122," Johnny continued. "It's no luxury spa or anything, but like Tess said, anything helps."

Tess's mind spun at Johnny's words. How in the world would people bunk in a torn-down barn? Yes, an old concrete foundation and a wood pile was nowhere near to a luxury spa.

Anthony jumped up. "Not to change the subject or anything, but I've been pondering about the food situation since I heard. While Jessie's is a generous proposal, it sounds like we're talking numbers that would overwhelm her kitchen and even mine. But Mr. Stein's mention of my grandpa's old place got me thinking. The Grahams are famous for their family barbecues. We could round up a bunch of grills—not just the Grahams' but anyone who is willing to help cook—and take them out to the property, maybe get some donations of buns and meat from grocery stores here and in Duckdale Hollow as well as the food pantry, and try to feed anyone who shows up."

Discussion erupted in the room, people ironing out details and offering to make calls or gather food.

"I think that's an excellent idea, Anthony," Sheriff Lockheart said. "In fact, I think we should designate Monroe Scott's property headquarters every night around six. People can come for food and their housing assignment. What do you guys think?"

Fern Perry spoke up. "My Cheyenne can get her friends together and organize games for the displaced kids tomorrow afternoon."

With ongoing discussion in clusters around the room, Tess noticed Johnny making a sneaky exit from the community center. She jumped up to intercept him.

Outside the main doors, Tess called after him. "Johnny?" He stopped but didn't turn around. "Please." Her voice broke as she spoke.

He slowly rotated to face her.

"Is Monroe okay?" Emotion choked her, leaking out her eyes.

Johnny smiled weakly. "Leave it to you to jump right to it. Shouldn't you be asking why he wasn't the one to come here, considering his connection with this community? Why he wasn't offering his place himself?"

His eyes were wild, looking everywhere but directly at her, but she stared at him until he returned her gaze. "Fine," he conceded. "I guess that is what you're asking me."

Fear squeezed her chest even tighter. She feared she would pass out from asphyxiation if he didn't spill it right then. "I heard about a casualty—one of the firefighters? Is it Monroe?"

Johnny closed his eyes as if hearing the question pained him. "We don't know." In his pause, he seemed to reassess. "*I* don't know."

Unable to speak, she allowed her wrinkled forehead and questioning eyes to do the asking.

Johnny sighed. "We were out on a line when a call came through about an injured hotshot. They needed the ship to pick him up, and they wouldn't have room for all of us and a stretcher, so Monroe and Ryan offered to go in after him." He shuffled, looking at his feet before looking back at her. "We thought it was going to be a simple in-and-out pickup, that he'd be back on the line with the rest of us within a couple of hours." Johnny swallowed. "We haven't heard from them since."

Black swirled around the periphery of Tess's vision. No, she would not allow herself to succumb to confusion, depression, or anything else. Not yet.

"When was that?" Her question came out in a whisper.

In the silence between them, Tess could hear the

scraping of chairs and the murmur of voices coming closer.

"Johnny, when did you last see him?" In her own ears, her heartbeat thudded louder than her question.

"Yesterday, 2 PM."

Over twenty-four hours before. Three simple words had never weighed so much.

"What about the helicopter? Surely, you've heard from them? Don't they have communication?"

Johnny nodded. "Sure, sure. The helicopter came back just fine. They had the coordinates of where they dropped them off. The problem is that now that area is covered in flames, and we can't get a hold of them men." He shook his head slowly. "Not a word."

She didn't have to wonder if this was typical protocol.

"Thank you, Johnny."

This couldn't be happening. Tess took deep breaths. Ava came to her side and looped an arm around her waist.

Chapter Sixteen

Being called in to work a few hours early had never felt so good as it did the day after Monroe's argument with Tess. Monroe spent the first few hours of the shift out on the line with the crew, satisfyingly building up sore muscles to the background music of the crass jokes of his crewmen, the grunts of physical exertion, and the thunderous cracking of the fire. Putting his all into the backbreaking work staved off the worst of his regrets over walking out of Graham's Pharmacy. He should have fought for a relationship with the woman who'd captured his thoughts and daydreams. He knew that now. But with their breakup so public, and it looking like he was at fault, he was willing to give that one to Tess. At least it wouldn't look like she'd been left again when it was her doing the dumping. Which was why he ignored her texts and calls. Ripping off a Band-Aid, he told himself. Ripping off a Band-Aid.

So when the call came in late in the afternoon about an injured hotshot, Monroe volunteered before anyone else could. The hotshot's supervisor had radioed in an approximate location, explaining that some large boulders broke loose and his man slid down rocky cliff, putting him in a position too dangerous for his men to retrieve. And that was when helitack rappellers were called in. They could be dropped in where no one could hike.

If they needed to use the Bauman Bag for the rescue, a victim on a backboard would take up too much space for more than three in the crew, including the one to stay on the helicopter to run the ropes. Besides, it didn't take more than two to do a simple rescue.

"Johnny, you got the crew if I take this one?" Johnny nodded and kept working while Monroe looked over his crew. "How about you, Ryan? You up for a rescue this morning?" Ryan was a hard worker, and his youth and energy would complement his own experience. "Reggie, spotter."

It took a while for the ship to come pick them up from the line, and even longer to find the correct site for the rescue. They'd known it wouldn't be easy with the information given when the hotshot supervisor radioed in, but spotting the injured hotshot from the air proved impossible.

"These are the coordinates given," Boomer, the pilot, informed Monroe when they got close. "But I don't see any good places to land." That wasn't a surprise, and the reason they made sure to have rappellers on the mission. "I'm thinking this is about the best we're going to get, Scott."

Their helicopter could only get so close between the rugged rock walls. Even with their two hundred-fifty-foot rope, they could only get partway there. They would have to hike down the rest of the way. H-8CM hovered at a dizzying height. He was used to the view, of course, in fact it gave him a thrill every time, but every once in a while, the ruggedness of the mountain cliffs left him feeling off balance.

Monroe opened the helicopter door in preparation for the rappel. "Thirty feet to the left," he directed Boomer and waited as the helicopter nudged over slowly. A few more minutes of fine-tuning, and they finally had it. It wasn't perfect, but it was the best landing space they were going to find out here. "Good. Can you drop a few more feet?"

He still couldn't see the injured hotshot, but with the thick vegetation at the bottom of the cliff, he didn't expect to. "Hold."

He gathered the rope in his hand. "Dropping ropes." Monroe dropped the ropes over the side, the orange weight pulling it down taut.

"You ready?" Monroe eyed Ryan who nodded his response.

"Let's do this," Monroe said to Ryan. Over the radio, he said, "Rappeller hooking up." He attached his carabiner to the rope, tugging to make sure his connection was safe. "Rappeller to the skid." He leaned back out of the helicopter, feet on the metal running board. "Rappeller off the skid."

Lowering himself through the wind and over the tops of the trees was the closest anyone could come to flying. The rush of the air gave him that shot of adrenaline he craved. What other job gave a man the opportunity to be a superhero? He just hoped they would find the hotshot soon enough to help him. They only had a few hours until dark, and if they didn't complete the rescue before then, the helicopter would be grounded until morning. Just in case, they prepared for an overnight with an injured man.

As soon as Monroe was down, Ryan followed.

"When we find him," Monroe told Reggie, "I'll radio up to tell you if we need the Bauman bag or the screamer suit."

Rappelling down into the secluded ravine was the easy part. They would have to traverse the rest of the arduous journey on foot. Monroe and Ryan called out for the injured man, trying to figure out which way to go. Using gravity as their best guide and splitting up only as far as they could still see each other but cover more ground, they searched.

"This is why every firefighter needs to be equipped with a GPS tracker," Monroe grumbled when he and Ryan met up for a water break. "Every minute it takes us to find this man could be jeopardizing this man's life."

The separated and continued combing down the ravine, each taking care not to become the next victim on the loose, rocky surface They'd been at it for nearly an hour already.

"Scott," Reggie's voice came over the crackling radio. "H-8CM is being called off on another mission. You good for a while?"

"Sure. I'll radio when we find him and assess the situation. Thanks, Reg."

The helicopter, now just a speck in the sky, left, but Monroe didn't worry that he would see it again soon. He just got back to the job at hand.

"Found him, Supe!" Monroe heard Ryan yell off to his right almost another hour later. By the time they attended to the man, whatever his injuries, it would already be too late for the helicopter to pick them up that night. "Over here!"

Monroe jogged down the steep incline, careful not to start a rock slide down the mountain. His quads burned at the sustained activity. "What have we got?" Monroe rushed to the hotshot's side and knelt down by Ryan who was already making an assessment.

"Probable broken ankle and compound fracture of ulna and radius."

Monroe's practiced eye noted the same. The man was in and out of consciousness. "Daniel?" Monroe tried to get his attention. Maybe it would be better to have him unconscious while they splinted him, but he didn't want to startle the man. "I see your left ankle and your right forearm injuries. Does anything else hurt?"

As soon as Monroe had a handle on the extent of Daniel's injuries, he radioed in. "Located injured hotshot." He read off his GPS coordinates. "Will have to transport him to a better location for pickup."

"H-8CM is still out on another mission, but we'll be back as soon as we can," Reggie said. "Get back to us when you have a more accessible position, and we'll let you know when we're back on their way."

They didn't have time for this. It would be dark soon.

"We need to find a place where Reggie can spot us when they come back," Monroe told Ryan. "And somewhere high enough up that the ropes can reach." This wasn't going to be easy, especially on Daniel, but with the bones splinted and two of them to help shuffle him along, they could do this. They didn't have any choice.

But Monroe was concerned. To say Daniel was in bad shape would have been an understatement. The man had not only tumbled down a rocky cliff, separating him from the rest of the crew and snapping a few key bones, he was severely dehydrated and in shock, making cardiac arrest a real risk.

Sure enough, by the time they managed to get Daniel comfortable on a relatively flat ledge away from trees and cliff faces, twilight prevented the helicopter's return. Odd thing was, when Monroe tried to relay their new position, radio communication wasn't going through. It didn't matter. Either way, they were in for a long night.

Monroe just didn't realize how long. They doped Daniel up as best they could to deal with the pain, and the three of them fell into fitful sleep.

"Supe!" Ryan's yell brought Monroe out of a deep sleep just before sunrise. He felt like he'd just fallen asleep, though it had to have been a good couple of hours.

Instantly, he was aware of the smoke that told him the fire was much closer than it should have been. Yesterday, the whole area had been in a safe zone—the only thing that kept their emergency situation from being dire—but the fire had jumped.

Without a word, Monroe and Ryan left their tarps, and grabbed their backpacks, each slipping an arm around the groggy Daniel, who moaned when they lifted him.

"We need you to help, Daniel," Monroe encouraged. "Just like yesterday. I know your good leg has got to be tired." Carrying the man on a backboard might have been easier on the victim, except that on this steep climb, that would have even been more impossible than the three of them struggling for every foot traveled.

Monroe looked over the side of the cliff to where they'd been the day before. Where Daniel had landed was now completely engulfed in flames, and they needed to get higher. The helicopter would never find them now with the ravine filled with smoke.

As they struggled up the embankment, Daniel's dead weight went unexpectedly off-balance, and Daniel flung out his good arm to grab onto Monroe. In the move, his uninjured hand slipped across Monroe's shoulder, knocking his radio from its holder, and in one horrible moment, they watched as the radio bounced down the cliff and into the fire zone. Their rescue just got exponentially more difficult.

The next several hours took everything they had to keep the three of them alive, away from the fire, and to a place where they could be discovered. In the end, it was H-8CM hovering overhead, unwilling to give up despite thick smoke and their probable demise in the fire, and Monroe's trusty pocket mirror that finally signaled their position. Twenty-eight hours after the original call, Reggie was lowering the scream suit for Daniel, and the three men were lifted out and then flown through the air in a short-haul rescue to a place where the helicopter could land and finish the transport.

The only good thing about it was that by the end of

the trip, his pack was significantly lighter with every morsel of food, drop of water, and stitch of medical supplies exhausted. And it would have been nice to have more.

Now back at base camp, recuperating in his truck for a moment, Monroe thought back over the ordeal. Because he had been able to snatch a few hours of sleep overnight, he really shouldn't be as exhausted as he was. The aftereffects of adrenaline rush might have something to do with the extreme fatigue, though at this point in his career, he'd thought himself immune. Then again, he'd never had a crisis call quite as intense as this before.

Monroe chugged his bottle of water and plugged in his phone, the battery dead for two or three days now. He leaned his head back into the headrest. It wouldn't hurt to catch a few winks in the afternoon sun. A lot had happened in his time away from base camp. When he returned, Monroe heard stories of Riverside's evacuation, the ensuing firefighting efforts, and even the rumor of a fallen firefighter—who, thanks to Monroe and Ryan and a merciful God—may have fallen, but didn't perish. While it probably ended the hotshot's career, he would eventually make a full recovery.

A twenty-minute power-nap elevated Monroe from feeling sub-human to just below passing. A shower and a hot meal would go a long way. Knowing he should probably walk back to base for a shower at least,

Monroe checked his phone first. There were a few missed calls—from his parents, his crewmen, and even a couple from Tess, which made his heart warm—and a handful of texts.

Unsure where to begin, he started with the voice mails. If Tess had called and texted multiple times, maybe she missed him as much as he missed her. Even in those exhausted, stressful moments as Ryan snored at his side and Monroe lay listening to the labored breathing of their fallen comrade, he wondered what Tess was up to. Perhaps she was showing houses or doing paperwork or stubbornly running ten miles in smoke thick enough to choke Smoky the Bear.

He pressed the play triangle on the newest of the voice mails.

"Monroe," Tess's voice shook. She was holding back emotion, and it made his chest constrict. "I don't mean to bother you again if the reason you're not picking up is because you don't want to talk to me." He heard her sniff. "But I know Johnny can't get a hold of you either, so now I'm really worried. They're saying—" She drew in a deep breath and let it out slowly. "Well, never mind what they're saying. Could you at least send me a text? Just tell me you're okay." She was definitely crying now. "I don't think I could handle it if you weren't." Another pause. "Please be okay," she whispered as if not even to Monroe.

Monroe looked at the time stamp. The frantic call

had been placed the day before. He raked a hand through his filthy hair and wiped his hand along his even filthier pants. He couldn't believe he'd put her through this. He turned his truck on and threw the transmission into drive. The shower and hot meal would have to be in Cobble Creek, because he needed to find Tess first.

He was a right fright, but Tess didn't deserve to worry one second longer than was necessary. In fact, he'd had her number cued up for a call before he decided that this reunion needed to be in person rather than over the phone. If she was truly that distressed, even thinking *he* was the one who had died, he needed to show her—flesh and blood—that he was fine. Smelly, but fine. He couldn't just spring it on her over the phone.

Making the drive to Cobble Creek at a pace that would get him there in half the time it should have taken, Monroe hoped law enforcement would be otherwise occupied. Barely inside the town line, Monroe pulled into a gas station to give his pickup at least a few gallons' cushion to find Tess. With the pump flowing, he leaned back on his truck, eyes closed to create a game plan for tracking down a certain redhead and smiled to himself. It would all work out.

"Monroe?" The sound of shock evidenced the woman thought it couldn't possibly be him.

His eyes flicked open. Was that Tess? He turned toward the voice.

"Ava?" He smiled. Close, but not quite. Still, she could direct him exactly where he needed to go.

Ava shoved a bag full of convenience-store snacks at Tyler who stood grinning at her side, and ran to Monroe, arms outstretched and ready to hug him.

He put his arms out to stop her. "I wouldn't do that if I were you."

"Oh, get used to it." She hugged him anyway. "I'm so glad you're okay. I was feeling awful about having to leave Tess when she's so distressed, but our residencies start in two days, but how could I leave Tess when—" She gulped. "But you're okay." She drew in a deep, shaky breath. "Have you talked to Tess yet?" Ava pulled her phone from her pocket. "She's—"

"Wait."

At Monroe's request, Ava dropped the phone to her side with a questioning look.

"I wanted to tell her in person. Where I can find her?"

Ava studied him for a moment, probably weighing the benefits of alleviating Tess's discomfort immediately and allowing Monroe to do it as he wanted.

"As a matter of fact, I do. She's at your place."

"My place?" Now if that wasn't confusing.

"Remember our agreement," Tyler called as he

opened the passenger door and handed the snacks to Glenn in the back seat.

"You got it." Monroe ignored Ava's questioning look and shot Tyler a thumbs-up. "Have a safe trip."

Chapter Seventeen

After the town meeting, Tess was dying to get over to Monroe's place, if for nothing else than to see what resources available to her, and that meant sucking it up and heading out to her grandfather's place to see what was left of the barn for her to work with. Johnny made it sound like perhaps something was there, but she didn't know if that meant more than a wide-open space that could serve as a makeshift campsite. Unfortunately, she was tied up in town gathering keys and lists and supplies, and by the time she headed out of Cobble Creek, a crowd would already be gathered there.

When Tess's SUV made the corner of the private drive on the property and broke through the tree line, she couldn't believe her eyes. Her grandfather's barn was still standing, and looking better than ever. Not new, by any means, but somehow, sturdier, and brightened up. Maybe that was a reflection of the lights and the energy of the people milling around. She was dying to go inside, to reassure herself with her own eyes that yes, the barn was still standing—for real—but she was overtaken by the mayor as soon as she stepped out of her vehicle.

"Food's ready, and we've started serving, so we need you to hand out housing assignments, if you could. Just be available, hang out in the food area and people will find you."

She grabbed her clipboard and the house keys, and made her way into the crowd to do just that. If nothing had changed inside the barn, it could house several families—except for the lack of adequate bathroom facilities, but it was a roof over their heads.

❁

Driving down the lane to his property, Monroe couldn't believe how much had changed in a few very long days. When he'd left, he'd been heartbroken but pleased with the progress on the barn. He had driven out ready to face a typical work week, knowing it would be hard, dirty, hot, and grueling but worth it. Little did he'd know, he'd get lost in the forest with a gravely ill patient who couldn't hike over the rocky terrain of his own power. And he had no idea that outside the eye of his own personal hurricane, the fire would spread to affect so many, displacing them from their homes, and that people would be mourning a loss that never actually happened. And yet somehow, his own little oasis in the mountains had become headquarters for it all.

Among dozens of other vehicles, Monroe found a place to park in the near dark, and took a few moments looking in from the outside, observing the throngs of people close to the barn under the floodlights. A mixture of Cobble Creek residents—more than a few of which he recognized—and several displaced families mingled. They cooked, served, and accepted meals, chatting and laughing as if this were normal. The scene looked like a cross between the biggest family reunion he'd ever seen and a county fair.

He kept looking around until there, off to the side, he finally spotted his redheaded beauty, locks in waves flickering like fire around her shoulders, a clipboard in one hand and a pen in the other, contentment on her face as she took in the crowd. She had something to do with this gathering on his property, and he couldn't be prouder. What was more, with the loving look on her face, she would never convince him she didn't like these people or their small-town camaraderie. She was just as much a part of it as anyone else.

If Ava's reaction was any indication what he might be up against with Tess, perhaps warning her would be better than completely springing it on her. Monroe wouldn't turn down her arms being flung around his neck—it made a great fantasy, in fact—but if that meant she'd have a heart attack at seeing him . . .

He did have to admit it felt good to know how much Tess cared, though. Over the weeks, Monroe had gone from knowing there was nothing between them, to a quest for fun, and then on to a sliver of hope. Dangerously, he'd started to care for her, but the façade had shattered. But now, with the voice mail and Ava's reaction as proof, Monroe couldn't help but hope this was it.

Still watching from afar, Monroe dialed Tess's number, watching her look of realization when she must have known the call was from his phone.

"Monroe?" she asked with no hello. "Is that you?" She hugged the clipboard to her chest.

"It's me. I'm okay," he was quick to say. "I'm so sorry you had to go through that."

"You're okay." Her breath hitched as she must have suppressed a sob.

He heard her contented sigh, and watched her shoulders rise and fall comfortably back down. It was a different experience being able to see the phone call at the same time.

He walked closer to her, but still on the outskirts of the property, just inside the tree line where no one would see him. When she saw him, he wanted their reunion to be private.

A couple seconds of silence ticked by. Was that all she had to say? Monroe was starting to feel dumb. She had said all she wanted was to know he was okay. She hadn't said she wanted him back. He had created that whole scenario.

She wiped her cheek on her shoulder sleeve. It might have been sweat—it was August after all—but the fact that it might have been something else, gave him the courage to continue.

"I needed to see you . . ." *I sound like an idiot.* "I couldn't wait any longer."

"Do you mean . . ." Tess started looking around at faces in the crowd.

"Yes. Five o'clock."

He smiled as she whirled around, and his heart took off.

Chapter Eighteen

It took a moment for Tess's eyes to adjust to the filtered shadows of the trees especially in the quickly approaching dusk. To distinguish the soot-covered man, with his black T-shirt and dirty cargo pants, from the landscaping was nearly impossible.

As soon as their eyes connected, though, she allowed her arm to lower the phone. She slid it back into her pocket, and with a smile and her eyes locked on his, she walked quickly, purposefully toward him. How she wanted to run, but she also didn't want to attract anyone else's attention. Selfishly, she wanted him all to herself.

At the edge of the clearing, Tess threw her arms around his neck, burying her face into the space right under his ear. "You're okay." Tears pricked at her closed eyes. "You're okay." She would never let him go.

Monroe picked her up off of her feet, still in the

THE COMBUSTIBLE ENGAGEMENT

embrace, and carried her a few yards away into the privacy of the trees. "I'm so sorry, Tess," he whispered over her shoulder, extending their embrace for a few more seconds before setting her back down.

"If you hadn't told me where to find you, I never would have recognized you. With this—" She rubbed his stubbly face and left her hand there while she continued. "I would have thought you were one of the unfortunate refugees who left in such a hurry, he didn't even have access to a razor and has been sleeping in a tent."

Monroe turned his head enough to press a kiss into her palm. "Something like that."

"I can't believe it." She couldn't tear her eyes off him. "I'm so glad you're okay. I'm so happy you're back." One of tears she'd been holding back for far too long leaked out, and this time it was he who reached out.

Cradling her face in the palm of his hand, he wiped her tear gently away with his thumb. At his touch, the touch she had dreamed about for days, Tess closed her eyes for the briefest of seconds, and when she opened them again, Monroe was hovering, his lips just over hers as if waiting permission. He didn't have to ask.

Tess pressed her lips to his, surprised by the softness next to the rough stubble of his cheeks. She kissed him hungrily, allowing every worry to evaporate in every fulfilled dream of being together. They were together because they wanted to be, not because she'd said they were.

Monroe pulled her closer, wrapping his arms all the way around her, and she was grateful for the solid reminder that he was here. He was fine. He was hers.

As much as she'd enjoyed that kiss on Main Street a couple weeks back, this was their first real, alone kiss, and it was absolutely perfect. It didn't matter that he hadn't shaved and smelled like he'd been at a bonfire for days. His clothes were probably soiling hers as she pressed against him. But none of that mattered. He'd come back for her.

Tess never wanted to stop kissing him, but she was supposed to be around to give out housing assignments. Now that Monroe was back though, and his welcome home a big success, maybe there would be more time to explore this side of their relationship in the near future.

Reluctantly, Tess ended their kiss. "I need to get back, but . . ." The look in his eyes drew her back in for a shorter peck. "I'm so glad you're back." She kissed him again. "I think I might have said that." She flushed but was unsure why admitting that might embarrass her.

"You need to be pretty clear with me," Monroe joked, "because sometimes smoke gets in my eyes."

"Come on." Tess grabbed Monroe's hand and was determined to never let go. "I wonder if anyone brought marshmallows." Whether she tasted ash when kissing Monroe, or it was just the smoky smell that permeated from every bit of him, she wasn't sure, but whatever it was, the kiss had been worth it. "For some reason I have a hankering for roasting marshmallows."

She pulled him back to the rest of the crowd. Was it just Tess or was the evening more beautiful than it had been the night before? The sky was no clearer. Smoke obscured any traces of constellations. Even the moonlight had to fight its way through the thick haze, filling the clearing with the feeling of Halloween in August. But everything else was so much clearer—at least to Tess.

The air smelled of hamburgers cooked just right and ears of corn grilled to perfection. The chatter among the people resembled a happy garden party rather than of people in the throes of depression and worry over missing the comforts of home. The lines at the grills were slowing, and everyone looked content.

"I bet it's nice to have your fiancé back," Connie from the salon commented as Tess and Monroe rejoined civilization.

"Yes, it is." She smiled and squeezed Monroe's hand.

He only had a surface understanding of that comment, especially coming from Connie, but she had been there when Tess first found out she might never see Monroe again. It was nice to live in a small-town community. To be among people who knew she'd been struggling. People who had been there to help her through an extremely tough time, and now that the crisis was past, to share in her joy.

Tess leaned into Monroe, loving the feel of pulling her hand toward her so he would lean closer. "Should we tell people we were never really engaged?" she whispered.

"Not yet, if that's okay with you." His breath on her ear sent goosebumps down her arm. "Let me enjoy this first."

After several claps on Monroe's back and even more exclamations of *welcome home*, Monroe looked around at the group sprinkled across his property. "Are you in charge of this event?" He looked at Tess. "Because I have some news they might be interested in."

"Just whistle or something." Tess pushed away the notion that she was in charge of anything with a wave of her hand. "They'll gather. You don't need me."

She felt him press her hand with a slight squeeze. "You'll never convince me of that." Her insides melted with that statement, but he was already calling everyone together.

"I have some good news. Nothing official yet or anything, but as of when I left base camp an hour ago, the fire near Riverside is under control. And—" He paused, making people strain for what would come next. "So far, no structures have been affected."

A few whoops filled the space between his sentences, and Monroe smiled, allowing them to celebrate. "Keep an eye on Twitter for the official word of when you can get back into your homes, #WolfRidgeFire, but I'm happy to say, it is going to be sooner rather than later." The crowd erupted into more cheers.

"Until then, you're welcome to stay on my property... oh wait, you're already doing that." He looked at Tess at his side and squeezed her hand again. "But I might give you a hammer in the morning and make you work for your stay." He got a few laughs from the crowd. "How about a big hand for our community volunteers?" He raised Tess's hand between them, and the clapping grew.

Overwhelmed by their gratitude, Tess took over. "And Jessie and Trent Lockheart, and Anthony Marino, and Mayor Armstrong, and well, too many other people to mention."

Community. She was engulfed in the meaning of it. Protection. Help. Working together. Mourning with those who mourn. It brought tears to her eyes and peace to her soul.

"Speaking of the property," Monroe asked when everyone else had gone about their business. "What did you think?" He cringed as if anticipating a negative response.

"I'm surprised it's still standing, if that's what you mean." She smiled her gratefulness at him.

"What did you think about—" He stopped. "Have you been inside yet?"

Tess bit her lip and shook her head, her heart starting to thump hard in her chest. From the way he was acting, she anticipated a happy surprise.

"Yes!" Monroe fist-pumped and grabbed her hand. "Come on. Let me give you the grand tour."

He brought her to the front. "The front door will be one of the last things to go in, I understand. If those had been changed, or the new windows we're putting in up front, you might have already guessed what we're doing here." Monroe tugged on the barn door to reveal a wide entry into what could easily be . . . a living room?

Tess felt her eyes open wide with surprise. "Are you . . . is this going to be a house?"

Monroe breathed out a relieved laugh. "Yeah. Like it?"

Tess couldn't believe it. The place had a long way to go in its conversion, but the idea alone was fabulous. Retaining as much of the layout and charm of the old barn, horse stalls and hay lofts gave way to an open-concept living room and a master bedroom with a luxurious en suite bathroom and a huge walk-in closet.

"I love the matte black fixtures and the whole industrial style." Tess rubbed her hand over the white subway tile in the bathroom. He'd only started laying it the other day before he got called away the other day and had practically the entire room still to do.

They walked back out to the living room where the heavy wood beams remained overhead, with outside walls being insulated and in the process of being covered with wide-planked shiplap. "My favorite, though, is the brick." An interior wall and the fireplace were the perfect accent to all the wood.

"I thought you might like that," Monroe said, seemingly pleased with himself.

"And the laundry room?"

He took her down a short hall. "The Stegers are a little better at the plumbing than I am. Not to mention they have more time. Anyway, they're taking the primitive plumbing here already and are transforming it into two full spa-like bathrooms, a large laundry room, and the kitchen, of course."

"What are you doing with the hayloft?" Tess eyed the space that was as yet untouched.

"That is a surprise. I'll show you when it's finished."

"Hmm. I like surprises." Did that mean he was expecting the two of them to stay together long enough for her to see the completion of the home. It would take several more weeks, maybe even months to finish the project.

"So now that you've seen it, what do you think?"

Tess stopped and faced Monroe, taking both of his hands in hers. "It is going to be gorgeous. I love what you're doing here. You have exquisite taste, and I love the reclaimed wood."

"I thought you might." His smile made her heart soar at being able to share this with him.

"And the best part? Well, it's kind of hard for me to decide, but... thank you. Thank you for not destroying this piece of my childhood. Someday, some other family is going to get as much enjoyment out of this old place as I did growing up, and that means a lot to me."

Monroe leaned down, his lips so close to hers, she could feel his warmth. "You're welcome."

At his kiss, she melted into him, safe in each other's arms.

Chapter Nineteen

Two Months Later

Tess stamped snow off her feet on the new front patio. She inspected the gorgeous new lanterns flanking the double front doors as she waited for Monroe to answer her knock. She was answered by one or two more pops of the nail gun. As far as she knew, Monroe was finishing up the wide baseboards. The air compressor hissed down, and Monroe's footsteps echoed closer as he came to greet her. It was a good thing she'd texted to alert him of her arrival because he never would have heard her knock.

He opened the door with a smile and she reciprocated with a steamy cup of vanilla hot chocolate, something new her dad had the staff at the soda counter trying out. He took the cup but paid it no attention, focusing instead on giving her a thorough good morning kiss.

When she had her wits about her again, she looked around at the minimally furnished, almost finished home. Monroe had been living here when he was not out on a job, which had meant he'd been there for a month straight at least.

Every time Tess stepped through the double mahogany doors at the front of Monroe's house, she was blown away by the progress. The place had long since left the department of "Grandpa's barn" and was quickly becoming Tess's secret dream home, though she called it Monroe's. That was what the deed said.

Brick beams and arches grew from the pre-existing horse stalls, creating a separation from the entry hall and the great room. Paired with another brick wall on the opposite side and natural wood beams and boards created the ceiling, the fireplace surround Monroe had crafted from reclaimed wood looked amazing under the industrial-style lights. At the other end of the great room sat a deliciously open kitchen with an oversized island, soapstone counters, and the perfect balance between doored cupboards and open shelving. It wasn't the style she had pegged Monroe with when they'd gone house hunting together, but it fit him perfectly— and the home he'd built far exceeded her expectations.

"With the snowfall, this fire season will be officially over," Monroe said, leading her into the kitchen. Carefully, he took the hot chocolate cup from her hand, and placed both cups on the island. "Which means it's time to celebrate."

Intrigued, Tess followed his lead toward the floating staircase. "The railing turned out absolutely beautiful." Tess ran her hand over the iron railing. While far more rustic than she would have imagined, she was starting to think that industrial must be her taste.

"I think so too," Monroe said. "Frank Lawson welded it on site for me."

He started to lead her up the stairs, but Tess paused before placing her foot on the first tread.

"You're letting me go upstairs?" She quirked an eyebrow at him. Until this point, the second story had mysteriously been off-limits.

Rubbing his stubbled chin, Monroe pretended to mull over the potential consequences and then nodded. "It's time."

Anticipation fluttered through Tess as she rose. Seeing the great room below her from this height was even more impressive. It was astounding what Monroe had accomplished by adding a few touches to the existing structure, yet it had transformed from an outdoor work space to a cozy home.

But when she reached the landing at the top of the stairs and the loft space opened up to her view, Tess could focus on nothing else. A large window filled the space where the hayloft door had been, a wide window seat underneath. Bookshelves filled every last inch of the back wall, even up into the peak of the ceiling. There was just enough room for a small desk and a couple of comfortable chairs with ottomans between the shelves and the railing that overlooked the rest of the house. Tess had spent many hours in this hayloft as a child, often with a book in hand, and she could think of no other place on earth she would rather spend her time as an adult.

"In my mind, I was going to show you this room when it was completely furnished and the bookshelves filled," Monroe spoke from behind her.

Unable to look away from the gorgeous structure, Tess stepped over the compressor cord to run her fingers over the wooden shelves.

"But then I realized that to do that, I'd need access to your books."

Was he saying what she hoped he was saying?

Tess turned to tell Monroe how gorgeous the loft library was even without the books, only to find him down on one knee. He was holding a dazzling cushion-cut solitaire set in yellow gold and her breath caught in surprise.

"Tess, ours might not be a fairy tale or classic romance, but our love burns as bright as Darcy and Lizzie's or Beauty and the Beast's. I may have let you go once, but once I knew I had a chance, there was no way I wouldn't come back and reclaim my bride—if you'll have me." He swallowed, and Tess couldn't believe what she was hearing, what she was feeling. "Tessa Jane Graham, will you marry me?"

"Yes!" Tess pulled Monroe up with both hands so she could communicate with her kiss how she felt about his question. She started with a sweet kiss, her lips barely touching his, but his response got her heart thumping. Her fingers rubbed across his cheek stubble, her thumb landing just in front of his ear as her fingers delved into the dark waves of his hair. She could enjoy the feel of his lips on hers for the rest of her life, and she was looking forward to it.

After a few delicious moments, she pulled back. "But does that mean we have to tell people we haven't really been engaged all this time?" she teased. They never had set the town straight.

"Just let them think I was slow in buying the ring. Blame it on Tyler." He slipped the ring onto her finger.

"Tyler?" She almost couldn't think about him as she watched sunlight refract through the brilliant diamond.

"Yes. He and I chose these rings together. He told me we needed to get on with the engagement because Ava was getting a little impatient."

Tess looked back up at him, feeling the question on her brow. "Am I supposed to know what you're talking about?"

Monroe laughed. "Tyler wanted to give me the

chance to propose first—seeing as how that's what started all this to begin with."

Tess felt her face flush. "Did he know?"

"That we were never engaged?" Monroe's lips lifted to a half smile. "Before you even told Ava, though he didn't say anything to her. It's a guy thing. He knew. Anyway," he pulled his phone from his pocket, "I need to let him know you said yes so he can finish his plans for his own proposal tonight." He tapped out a quick text to Tyler and deposited the phone back into his pocket before wrapping his arms around her again. "I think I'm going to like having a brother. Finally."

"And another sister?" Tess teased.

He shrugged. "Part of the package deal." He nuzzled Tess's neck, making her forget what they were even talking about. "So what do you think of the house? Did I do okay, or do we need to put it back on the market and start over?"

His hot lips were on hers, keeping her from having to answer a completely rhetorical question. She'd found her man. The one who had built this home for her. The one who loved her.

Acknowledgments

I always have so many people to thank in assisting me to get a book to publication—this one especially. There is no way I could have written a book about wildland firefighting without advice from people who work in the field.

Thank you to Jason Porter for your patience. You answered numerous questions from someone you'd never met. All of my details were founded on the information he generously offered. Thank you also to the Lewiston Interagency Helitack Facebook group for answering random questions from an author who stumbled onto your page.

Another huge thank you to Daniel Coleman, not only for your expert content editing that made this book so much better, but also for offering your own wildland firefighting experience. How lucky I was to be paired with you!

Thank you to my cousin, Jeremy Clark, for relating his experience in being evacuated from his home due to California wildfires.

One last very important thank you to my young friend Maggie. I appreciate your book suggestions; I hope you didn't mind me borrowing your name for my character.

About the Author

When Maria Hoagland is not working at her computer, she can be found combing used furniture stores and remodeling houses with her husband. She loves crunching leaves in the fall, stealing cookie dough from the mixing bowl, and listening to musicals on her phone.

Maria has several published works in the sweet romance and women's fiction genres, including two Whitney Award finalists. She enjoys hearing from readers and book clubs and can be found online at mariahoagland.com.

For updates on new releases and a free copy of the novel *Kayaks and Kisses* or the Spellbound in Hawthorne bonus short story, *Recipe for Disaster,* sign up for Maria's newsletter on her website.

facebook.com/mariahoaglandauthor

twitter.com/MariaHoagland

instagram.com/mariahoagland

bookbub.com/authors/maria-hoagland

pinterest.com/mariahoagland

Next in Cobble Creek

Thank you for reading *The Combustible Engagement*. That's officially the end of the Cobble Creek series, but I couldn't leave this idyllic town for long. Return to Cobble Creek for Christmas with soccer player Camden Sharpe.

Santa Cam

The one behind the camera could be his best match yet.